CEREMONY OF FLIES

CEREMONY OF FLIES

by

Kate Jonez

Omnium Gatherum
Los Angeles

Ceremony of Flies © 2014 Kate Jonez

ISBN-13: 978-0692446690
ISBN-10: 0692446699

This book is a work of fiction. Names, characters, places and incidents are either the products of the author's imagination or are used fictitiously. Any resemblance to actual events or persons, living or dead, is coincidental.

Trade Paperback Edition

For Kristine

ONE

"Seems to me like maybe you ain't happy inside. Maybe you liked it better working the door." Mort shoves his glasses up the bridge of his nose with his thumb.

Mort is a big man who'd heard too many stories about the good old days of Vegas. He's like a walking, talking, black-and-white gangster movie, but for real.

Not really for real, but *he* thinks he's for real. His twenty-dollar-a-bottle cologne stinks like he's real.

I'm not happy inside.

I almost laugh out loud. Mighty insightful there, Mort. No scholar ever said truer words.

I don't care.

I do not fucking care if I stand outside or not. It's humiliating, sure, smiling and waving and posing for pictures with the tourist losers. Working inside is no picnic either. What the fuck does it matter what piece-of-shit job I do to amass the few lousy dollars I need to keep the pay-by-the-week roof over my head.

Does not matter to me.

A fly buzzes past my ear and lands somewhere in the hairspray and carbon-based tangle known as my hair. I hear its hum like background music.

"No, I like working inside," I say, because that's what he expects me to say. It's the meta-dialogue. I know my part in this twenty-first-century pseudo–passion play. I pull my lips into a sexy little pucker that feels as stupid as it probably looks to prove to Mort that I mean what I'm saying. Or at least if the lie shows on my face, maybe he won't notice.

Sid's dulcet vocal stylings blast from the speakers. I can't see him, but there's no mistaking it's him. He's doing a number on Bon Jovi or Journey. It's hard to keep it straight.

Sid Delicious.

Some people have no shame.

In spite of the chill wind of the air conditioning, the cheap gold-colored rayon dress with the excessive purple ruffles clings to my skin. Clings where it shouldn't, that is, and itches everywhere else. The metal pins that hold my feathered and bejeweled headdress in place gnaw at my scalp. They're supposed to poke into my bouffant and stay put. That's what my co-workers say, anyway. But no matter how much I tease that damned wig and spray it and tease it some more, the spikes always try their best to weasel their way into my brain. All I need is a bit in my mouth and I'll be all set for shock therapy. A zap might be just what I need, come to think of it. Supposed to get rid of all the short-term memories. I've got some images in my head I could live without. Although, I suspect there is no way to get the worst of the worst stuff out. If I couldn't drink it away, and I damn sure gave drinking my best shot, there's probably no way some little surge of electricity would do the trick. Looks like I'm stuck remembering all the fucked-up shit in my life. Every little detail.

One of the slot machines sputters, coughs, and shudders like it's having a seizure. It vomits its guts out as sirens wail, horns blow and lights flash. People shriek like it's the end of the world.

It's not.

Midwesterners in shiny new khaki shorts and plaid shirts bought just for their Vegas vacations crowd around the machine to see who's been bitten by the luck bug.

Some poor old cow in a motorized cart, who by the looks of her hasn't leaned so low in several years, is struggling to get all her quarters into her bucket. The bland-looking folks crowding around her look like the kind of people who would help her if she asked. But she doesn't.

Forty-seven dollars and fifty cents, the sign on the slot machine flashes. Seems like a lot of fuss for that kind of money. Guess it'll buy a lot of cat food, though. Maybe a nice new pair of stretch pants.

When I was a kid, a woman used to ride one of those motorized carts up and down our street on garbage day. She'd poke at the garbage and sometimes even turn over a can or two. I forget what the kids called her, but I'm sure it wasn't flattering.

Gross old cow.

Every time she'd see me she'd shake her fist and yell about how things were bad because the Americans owed my people, the Chinese, so much money. She'd call me a communist too.

Whatever, bitch. Pay your bills.

In retrospect, I can see this behavior was dementia related. When I was a kid, though, I hated her so much. I wanted to grab a stick or a baseball bat and bash in her face. I actually used to daydream about it. I guess even as a kid I was rotten, but who the hell was she to call me Chinese in front of everyone? She made the kids on the street look at me like I was weird. She made them notice I was different. I hated her so much. I really wanted to kill her so bad. I was glad when she died and nobody found her for two weeks.

Really glad.

The people clutch their coin cups and wander back to their favorite machines. Wheel of Fortune, The Price is Right, Family Feud. Seems like they could save the plane fare and just stay the fuck home and watch TV.

"And your ashtrays haven't been shined."

Oh right, Mort's giving me a talking to. I hope I didn't miss anything important. My ashtrays do indeed lack shine. I nod that I understand.

Yellow, purple, and green lights flash and chase each other down the length of the bar. Those are the theme colors here at the casino. Beads and feathers and outlandish masks adorn every surface like the place is a worn-down dancer trying to cover her wrinkles with an extra layer of makeup. The whole place is done up like Mardi Gras and maybe that's a good choice. Feels like Lent is just around the corner most days.

Lent, motherfuckers, Lent.

Mort hitches his belt up over the lower-most bulge of his belly.

Aren't you natty, big boy? I hear front-butts are going to be all the rage this fall.

Mort scrubs at the cheap ashtray with the rag he has perpetually draped over his shoulder. He holds it up for me to see as if he were showing me a bug trapped in amber.

"Like this. Nice and shiny."

I narrow my eyes, which I try never to do because even though I look like I'm Chinese, I'm not. And squinting just reminds people to ask me stupid shit like if I'm good at math or can say something in Chinese or if my pussy slants the other way.

I'm not, I can't, and it doesn't.

I grew up in upstate New York with parents the color of paste in the most homogenized of white neighborhoods imaginable. So, I listen to hip-hop, eat bagels, drink coffee from South America and can't find the Middle East on a map, just like you, round-eye.

The purple ruffles adorning my cleavage catch a hefty gust from the air conditioner and expose my boobs for a second. They're covered only by see-through netting.

A red-faced Midwestern turd in a blue polo shirt his wife obviously bought for him twists his head and gawks.

Keep your eyes in your head, asshole. What's your problem? Never seen humiliation before?

Some other guy is propped up on a stool at the bar riding it like it's a mechanical bull about to take off. He's wearing a T-shirt with cigarettes rolled up in the sleeve as if he's Nicholas Cage playing Elvis or something. He grins when the red-faced guy's wife smacks his stupid fat head. The guy at the bar looks taut, like he works out. Not too bad at all. He salutes at me like he knows who I am.

I'm pretty sure he doesn't.

He winks and smiles a lopsided smile that's nice enough. Something is weird about his nose, it's crooked like it's been broken, but it doesn't ruin his face. In fact it makes it more interesting, masculine.

When Joey's nose got broken, it never healed right. I swear I channeled the ghosts of the blows that smashed his face when I looked at him. I could feel little shadows of the pain every time. His face was always so delicate and fragile. It was a shame his nose got broken.

Mort twitches his head, jowls jiggling, in the guy's direction. "Customer."

"What do you think he wants?" I smile at Mort, disgusting as he is, and make my extra-sexy face just for good measure.

Mort scowls, which changes his face very little. His mom should have told him it would stay that way. "You're going back on the door, missy, if you don't straighten up and fly right."

I snatch up my tray and somehow I don't spill the highball glass stuffed with dollar bills and assorted change. What I really want to do is smash it over Mort's head.

But I don't.

"You treat the customers right and they'll do the same."

Mort clamps his fat cigar between the yellow pegs of his teeth and points the V of his fingers to his eyes. "I'm watching you."

Cliché much?

I fight to keep my eyes from rolling as I totter across the threadbare Harlequin-patterned carpet. I hate these stupid fucking shoes. I go up to the guy at the bar.

"Hi there."

He smells like a guy ought to smell. Like smoke with a sharp splash of liquor and something earthy and dirty like motor oil. Up close I can tell he'd been in his share of fights. The last one probably hadn't been too long ago from the look of the purple smear across his sharp jaw. A shiny keloid ridge adorned with rows of ancient stitching follows the line of his eyebrow.

Fighting is completely awesome. Every single bit of everything is focused, sharp and truly alive. Nothing else comes close. Singing maybe. Sex, when it's good.

"You ever tried the deep-fried Twinkies?" His voice is gravelly from too much smoking. He sounds much older than he looks. Pretty sexy.

I balance my tray on my hip. "Is that what you want?" I listen to the buzz of a fly somewhere deep in the labyrinth of the hair and feathers piled on my head. I wonder if something died in there.

His smile looks like he's about to tell a joke. "I didn't say I wanted one. I asked if you ever tried one."

There's something about him that seems comfortable already. It's a weird déjà vu feeling. Maybe we met in another life. I don't believe in that shit, but the feeling is weird.

"Yeah, I've tried one." I can feel Mort watching me, so I take a pen out of my glass and pretend to write something on my tray.

"Well?" he says.

I look into his eyes. He's got lashes that are too long for a dude, like maybe he used a little mascara. His teeth are too bright to be real. But I like the way his hair falls down over one eye, like he planned it that way. Like he knows he looks good.

"To be honest, you'd think something as good as a Twinkie would be even better fried. But the truth is"—I lean in close and breathe in his scent—"fried Twinkies are disgusting."

"Whoo! Whoo!" He rocks back on his stool, grabbing the seat like the bull is about to start bucking and he's afraid he's going to fall off.

What the fuck? Ugh, what if he's a retard? I did not say anything funny.

I cast a sideways glance in Mort's direction. He's still watching. Doesn't he have some money to count or something?

"So you want a fried Twinkie?"

"I'll have a boilermaker. You know what's in that?" He winks again.

Maybe it's a nervous tic.

"Yep," I say as I move over to the side of him and lean against the bar to get his drink. "Boilermaker," I call out to the bartender.

"You'd be surprised how many people don't." He rubs his hands on his thighs like he's wiping something off. His hand grazes me.

Does he expect me to think that was an accident?

"Mixology is a fine art. A craft a man can be proud of," he says with a know-it-all smirk.

"We're professionals around here."

It's a shot dropped in a beer, dick-wad, not the Mona fucking Lisa. I smile at him but I'm not feeling it so much anymore. There's really no reason for me to get this guy's drink. He's sitting at the bar after all. But I take the glass from the bartender and set it on my tray.

"Hey. You think in a while you can show me where a guy can get a decent burger around here?" He's making eye contact. Really making eye contact like he wants to sell me a stolen car or something. I get a little tickle in my gut like something shifty is up. This guy works the angles. I can tell by the tone of his voice and his hypnotist's gaze. That's not necessarily a bad thing. Who doesn't work an advantage every now and then?

He better not think I'm some stupid mark.

I am not.

No idiot cowboy, Elvis-wannabe motherfucker is going to get one over on me. He's going to have to come up with something better than that. How is it even possible that he can't find what he wants in *Vegas*? I'm going to figure out what's up with him. Two can play this game.

"I guess." I watch him. His eyes aren't wandering over me like he's trying to figure out how much I'll charge for a blow job. So that's something.

I'd charge him twenty. He's good-looking. Or maybe fifty, because *Whoo! Whoo!* seriously?

"Don't think you're going to pull anything on me," I say. "It won't work." If he's trying to snuggle up and get the goodies for free, I will fuck him up.

He gets a surprised look on his face like no one has ever called him on his bullshit before. His mouth opens to say something at the same moment the red-faced Midwestern prick snaps his fingers in my direction.

I twist when I hear the sound and totter on my shoes. The drink still on my tray sloshes a little. The guy at the bar grabs my elbow to steady me.

Fucking shoes.

That Midwestern dick is going to be seriously lucky if I don't take off one of these glittery spiky monstrosities and bash in his head with it.

I stomp over to his table. I can feel the heat rising up inside me. "You really know how to snap those fingers, don't you?"

"I was trying to get your attention," the red-faced man says.

"No shit. I kind of got that impression."

His face turns an even darker shade of red. Let's go for purple, shall we? I lean over real slow and put my face down close to his. In my coldest, hardest mean girl voice I say, "What-do-you-want."

It's not a question.

He knows it.

"Is there a problem here?" Mort plasters a smile on his face that looks about as cheap as the Mardi Gras beads waitresses are supposed to give out.

"This asshole snapped his fingers like I'm some kind of dog."

Aaaand we've got purple. Better cool this boy down before he has a coronary. I drizzle the boilermaker over his head. The little shot glass falls out. Clunk. Right on his big old bald head. His stupid wife gets all flustered. Her hands fly up to her face. Just the reaction I'd hoped for.

Behind me I can hear the guy laughing, *Whoo! Whoo!*

Mort reaches out like he's going to grab me. I snatch my arm away and start to do some serious teetering on my ridiculous shoes. "Don't put your hands on me. I will stab you."

The words ring out as loud as the bell for the 10K jackpot.

Fuck.

I should not have said that.

I don't have words to describe the look on Mort's face.

"You know what, Mort. Don't even say anything. You're right. This isn't the place for me." I jerk the headdress off my head. It snags on my hair and makes my eyes water.

Now it fucking wants to stay in place.

With an extra hard tug I pull it free and shove it at Mort. "I quit."

Mort's eyes grow large behind the thick greasy lenses of his glasses. He should be glad I quit. It saves him having to fire me. So why's he just staring like that?

I want to go. It's time to go, but something about the way Mort's looking at me keeps me frozen in place. A single fly hovers in place between us. Slowly, like an ice sculpture melting, like the shift of a tectonic plate, his head tilts down. I follow the trajectory of his eyes.

A mysterious, inexplicable substance seeps, like soup on a carpet, into the taut white fabric stretched over his belly. A red Rorschach blot in the shape of a heart expands and spreads.

The pins, the torture devices designed to hold my head-dress in place, as long and as sharp as hypodermic needles, are stuck into Mort's shirt. If the horrified look on Mort's face is any indication, the spike holding the crown jewel has found its way into his heart.

Fuck.

The sounds of Bon Jovi or Journey wavers and warbles until it turns into a buzz like a swarm of flies. The *Whoo! Whoo!* from the guy at the bar is noticeably absent.

That train has left the station.

As Mort's knees buckle and he heads for the floor, I jump down from the lofty heights of my shoes and do the only sensible thing.

Run.

LAS VEGAS

In prehistoric times, marshes receded from the Las Vegas Valley, leaving an arid, inhospitable desert behind. Millennia later, water trapped in labyrinthine geological formations underground spewed forth, creating an oasis.

Many years later, gold diggers on their way to San Francisco and Mormons expanding their empire from Salt Lake City vied to settle the patch of green, the Meadows in Spanish, Las Vegas.

On October 1, 1910, an especially harsh law that forbade all gambling, even the flipping of coins for purposes of decision making, inspired Las Vegas gamblers to take their games underground. With the help of secret passwords and officials willing to look the other way, gambling flourished.

By 1931, gambling was legal, and Vegas was booming. The gold diggers, in a substantially different guise, had won.

TWO

Fuck! Fuck! Fuck!

This is not part of the plan. This is some tangential alternate reality. I have been transported to some new coil of string in someone else's theory. Plus I've got no shoes and I'm wearing a green and purple dress that would put a Puerto Rican welfare queen to shame.

I slink back into the shadows of the basement level of the parking garage for the Cortez. I'm not kidding myself. I know I'm not hiding. I fucking glow in the dark. But it's empty down here. There're hardly even any cars.

It should be cooler in the darkness than it is. The air feels like the inside of a mausoleum, still and oppressive. I've really dug my own grave this time.

Fuck.

I listen for sirens or the shouts of police. All I can hear is muffled clatter and the blast of Downtown Vegas noise.

That's a good sign.

Maybe things aren't so bad after all. Maybe Mort's all right and he's shining ashtrays and giving out Mardi Gras beads because I'm not at my post.

Yeah, keep dreaming.

I should take the stupid dress off. Find some shoes. That's the first thing I need to do. That's how you solve a big problem. Break it down into little pieces. I only wish my heart would stop pounding in my ears so I could think and the tightness in my chest would let up so I could breathe.

Think—breathe.

Things aren't any worse than after me and Joey ran

away to New York and I tried out to be a singer in the Slipper Room. I was scared shitless that night. When I stepped up on the stage to audition, I had a panicky feeling like a wave was cresting over my head. I held my breath and walked right up to the mic anyway. The wave crested and the feeling receded. Whatever was going to happen was going to happen. I was pretty good. They even told me to come back. I would have too, if the situation with Joey hadn't gotten out of control. I wanted that job really bad.

Things aren't any worse now. They're about the same actually. Except this time I'm the one who killed somebody. Feels about the same.

Whatever is going to happen is going to happen.

I catch a glimpse of something moving in the dark cave of the stairwell. My heart jumps up into my throat.

A little black kid with a head full of unruly curls pokes his head out and stares right at me. He looks just like the kid who was always hanging around us back in New York trying to steal our food. Two dots of red glow from out of the darkness like a dog's eyes reflecting light. The kid sticks his tongue out, then turns and runs up the stairs. The sound of his footsteps echoes through the parking garage. Did that kid spit something at me? I could swear I saw something fly out of his mouth.

Just a kid. I relax a little. Just a kid.

I march up one sparse row of cars and down the next, glancing in car windows like that's what I'm supposed to be doing. I try the door handles. Nothing opens, but at least no car alarms go off. Do cars even have those anymore? I need a break right about now. I need to find an open window, an unattended suitcase.

Against the far wall parked sideways in two and a half spaces, I see an old-fashioned convertible the color of midlife crisis. Oh please, oh please, oh please, I chant to myself as I run to it.

Yes!

On the backseat is the saddest overstuffed suitcase I've ever seen. It's bulging like a bloated corpse and just barely held together with bungee cords and gray rope.

The car's got nice leather seats and shiny chrome. The car and the suitcase don't match but I don't have time to think about that. The door's locked but the top is down so I reach in and unlock the door. Some real genius must own this vehicle. I climb in.

I snap off the bungee cord and tear at the knot in the rope. It gives and the guts of the suitcase spew all over the backseat. Right on top, I find pair of jeans that look about two sizes too big, but they'll work. There's flies close by, I can tell by the buzzing sound. This is exactly the kind of suitcase that would have something disgusting in it. If I plunge my hand into Fluffy's rotting corpse, I'll deal with it.

I toss aside some framed picture of an old lady and dig through the T-shirts and man panties until I find a white shirt with a collar and a monogrammed *B* on the pocket. Bet the guy is *Bill* or *Bob*. Maybe even a *Billy Bob*. A smell like smoke and liquor and something manly clings to the clothes. It reminds me of someone, but I can't put my finger on who. I don't really have time to worry about it anyway. My dress clings and scratches as I pull it off. I cannot think of one single piece of clothing I have ever been so relieved to be out of. I wriggle into the too-big jeans and thread the bungee cord through the belt loops. It would be a whole lot easier if my hands would stop shaking. Just as I'm buttoning up the shirt, I hear the tap of footsteps on concrete.

Fuck!

I drop down on the floorboard and hold my breath. Panic, like a wave in the ocean, rises up and grabs me, pulling me with it. I hold my breath to keep from drowning in it. The footsteps tap, tap, slow and determined, come my way. The wave of panic crests.

Whatever's going to happen is going to happen.

I exhale a little and a little more, not making a sound. The footsteps stop right by me. I'm afraid to look up, but I can feel eyes on me. I can feel the shadow of somebody standing over me.

"That's my good shirt," a familiar voice says.

My head turns up almost like gravity is pulling it. The guy from the bar is standing with his hand on the car. Not smiling exactly, but almost.

"Yeah, mind if I borrow it?"

"Looks like you're in a fix."

"You think?"

Is this fucking guy for real?

"Gimme that dress right there. The one you took off." He holds out his hand.

I grab it and toss it to him and without hesitating, like he planned it out ahead of time, he stuffs it in a drainage pipe. "Climb on up front."

"You're not going to call the cops?" I ask as I scramble over the seat and climb down on the floor.

He didn't even stop to think about his answer. "I gotta be in L.A. by morning. I can't see that me calling the cops is going to be good for anybody, what with me being a witness and all." He opened the back door of his car and a look of annoyance flickers over his face.

"Sorry about the mess. I was in a rush."

He packs all his stuff neatly back in the suitcase. He holds the picture of the old lady for a second before he closes the suitcase and puts it on top. He ties it with the gross old rope.

"Go ahead and get up off the floor."

He could move a little faster.

"You got money?" he asks as he slides into the driver's

seat. He's moving real slow like he's going out to cruise by the Sonic on a Saturday night.

So that's why he's helping me. It had to be something like that. I guess robbery is better than the rape-and-mutilation alternative.

"Yeah, I've got some." I don't get up. It feels safer down here. And it's remarkably roomy. Classic cars have that going for them. I think he's going to ask how much, but he doesn't. I don't have enough to get too excited about. Maybe fifteen dollars in tips stashed in the pouch tied around my waist and the credit card I nicked from the Midwestern prick's wife when I dumped the drink on his head. That should be good for a few thousand or so. They're on vacation, after all.

"Hey, Kitty, you ought to get up from there," he says again. "If you act like you done something wrong, people are going to think you did." He puts the key in the ignition. A little gold figure with a bald head and folded arms dangles from his keychain.

I hope that charm has some luck in it.

He's right though. If I'm hiding and looking scared and somebody sees me, they're going to know something's up. I climb up on the seat.

The car rumbles to life and as he's pulling out and rolling the car toward the exit, he reaches over in front of me and opens the glove box.

Whoa, that is not a glove. A blue-black weapon of deadly destruction lies casually in the glove box like it was posing as a checkbook or an old forgotten burrito. Right on top of it sits several magazines. He reaches past the gun and grabs a pair of mirrored sunglasses. He gives them to me.

Not really my style, but I put them on. I pull down the visor and smile at myself as he pays for parking and we roll out into the sunshine as bright as a spotlight pointed right on me.

THE JOSHUA TREE

Yucca Brevifolia is a treelike succulent native to south-western North America. It is found primarily in the Mojave Desert.

The name Joshua Tree was given to it by a group of Mormon settlers who crossed the Mojave in the mid-nineteenth century. The plant's unusual shape reminded them of the biblical figure Joshua raising his hands in prayer.

Good morning sister Mary
Good morning brother John
Well I wanna stop and talk with you
Wanna tell you how I come along
I know you've heard about Joshua
He was the son of Nun
He never stopped his work until
Until the work was done
God knows that Joshua fought the battle of Jericho
Jericho
Jericho
Joshua fought the battle of Jericho
And the walls come tumbling down

THREE

The desert spreads like a moonscape, unbroken in its desolate sameness all the way out to the curve of the earth. Joshua trees wave their twisted arms at the sky, like hopeless beggars grasping at the coattails of rich bastards. We fly down the freeway, riding a tiny string of civilization stretched like a high wire across overwhelming wildness.

I do not have a plan.

I did have a plan. I had the casino job by day, so I could audition at night. I had it all planned out perfect. I would work as a singer, use a fake name. It wasn't like the cops were going to look for me in Vegas for something that happened in New York. I wasn't even the main suspect. They just thought I was going to help them find Joey. Like that would ever happen. Joey and me are, were, too tight for that. Like it would even matter if they found him now. It was better to get out of town anyway. Vegas was great. My plan was great, although I should have landed a gig as many times as I tried out, but it's shot to shit, obviously. Now I've got nothing.

Damn.

I rub my sweaty palms on the legs of the too-big jeans. A billboard flashes past.

Accident? Injury? Legal Trouble?

I probably should call. Might as well.

Fuck!

I'm going to miss that audition this weekend. I'm way worse off that when I left New York. I'm so fucked. Where do I go from here?

"You sure nobody's following us?" I look over at Rex and ask again. That's his name. Yeah right, like his mother would name him that. It's been more than an hour since the last time I asked.

He looks in the rearview mirror, then leans over to check the side mirror. "Not that I can see."

I check behind us just to make sure. It looks clear, though there are a couple of cars that could be undercover cops. I don't really think they are. It feels like we got away. Like we time-traveled out of Vegas and slipped through the net. That's not the kind of luck I've been having lately. It doesn't feel like a sure thing.

"Doesn't that seem strange? Getting away so easy?"

"Ole Linda and me will get you where you're going. Don't you worry about that." He pats the dashboard like the car is a dog. "It's a sign." Rex looks over at me and grins. He's got some white damned teeth. "The Lord knows what you done was an accident and wants to give you a second chance." He sticks his hand in the pocket of his jacket. He leaves it there for a while moving his fingers around inside like he's playing with himself but I can't tell for sure.

"I think I should go to Mexico." Once I say it out loud, it makes a lot of sense. That's what people do, right? The guy in the *Shawshank Redemption*, Al Capone, Thelma and Louise. Once you stab a guy, Mexico's a place you ought to go. There's no going back after you do something like that.

"You speak Spanish?"

I shake my head. "I can learn."

"You know what *linda* means in Spanish?"

"It means *beautiful*. Everyone knows that."

He looks over with a weird expression on his face like he's disappointed that I knew, then turns back to look at the road.

"She is, you know. The '71 Pontiac GTO is the most *linda carro* ever made."

"Uh huh," I say.

He pats the dashboard again. "I'm taking real good care of you, Linda. Don't you worry. Nobody's ever going to take better care of you than me."

Whatever.

It's a car.

I seriously doubt *car-o* is Spanish for car, genius.

We fly along the freeway. All the emptiness zooms past in a blur as I imagine the hacienda I'll live in when I get to Mexico. I'm going to turn things around when I get there. Life will be good. I will be good. Yeah, like that's going to happen. The only thing being good ever gets you is screwed.

We come around some slight little curve in the otherwise straight road and a field of giant whirligigs appears like they were conjured by magic. They whip around and around. Miles and miles of them like giant whirling bugs trying to fly away.

"That is one *linda vista*," Rex says.

It *is* beautiful, the white blades beating against the endless blue sky. The sun's shining down and my hair is blowing out behind me. We're running and nobody's following us and it feels more free than free because I've got something concrete to compare it to. A vibration trembles in my heart, a concussion like wings beating inside me.

Rex's mouth hangs open a little like he's awed by the sight. Maybe we should hook up, I think. Maybe it'd be nice to travel with someone for a change. Someone to watch my back. Maybe he'd like it in Mexico.

He steers the car with one finger on the wheel and makes it glide over to the right lane.

Barstow, the sign flashes by.

He slows down to exit.

A hard fist of fear takes the place of the little wings in my heart. "What are you doing?"

"This is the halfway mark, Kitty. Gotta fuel up."

"I can't go to a city!" My heart is slamming in my chest

and I'm thinking about the mechanics of jumping out of the car.

"Don't worry none. Barstow's just barely a town. No time at all, you'll be on your way."

I take a deep breath. He's right. If they didn't follow me out of Vegas, they aren't going to be looking for me here. Nobody's looking for me. I might even be invisible, a nobody, just as I've always feared. My heartbeat slows to its normal pace.

Rex and me and Linda roll down the ramp into Barstow. He drives past the roadside McDonald's and Wendy's and into Barstow proper. The lawns are brown and crispy. The houses all seem to be the same exact shade of beige whether they're made of brick or stucco or wood. This does not look like a place where much happens. The word *sleepy* comes to mind.

"Can't you get gas back there by the highway?"

"Hey, Kitty, not to be rude or anything, but I think it's time we go our separate ways."

He turns into the parking lot of a shabby old shack with a sagging roof and a gas pump out front.

Crossroads Bar and Grill.

"Like I said, I gotta be in L.A. by morning and that probably isn't the best place for you, what with what happened and all."

He pulls the car up next to the gas pump and turns off the engine. I swear I can hear the *whoosh whoosh* of the whirligigs slicing through the air.

Of course. I should have known. He's probably a fag anyway or riddled with sexually transmitted diseases.

I get out of the car. Sharp pieces of gravel bite into the bottoms of my feet. I don't react to the pain. I'm not going to let him see my pain.

"Don't call me Kitty," I say. A tear trickles down my cheek. It's from the pain of the stones biting into my feet.

That doesn't count as crying. "What the fuck. My name is Emily. Em-uh-lee, got it?"

Over by the door to the Crossroads Bar and Grill, there's a little light-skinned black kid with a big nest of hair that looks as dusty as Barstow. He's maybe five or six and he's hanging on to the ugliest dog I've ever seen. It may be the ugliest *creature* I've ever seen. Except for a giant banana slug, that's uglier. But it's definitely the ugliest mammal.

"I didn't mean nothing by it, Emily."

Rex says my name all smooth like that's going to make me like him again, then he winks.

Give me a fucking break.

"Like I was saying, L.A. may not be the place you want to go. You just stay out of the way down in Mexico and soon enough they'll forget all about it."

The boy and the dog look forlorn like they're the last two souls on earth. They're watching me. The kid sticks his tongue out. A fly buzzes around the cave of his mouth. I want more than anything to throw a rock at them.

But I don't.

It's so much worse, this humiliation, so much worse with those two extra sets of eyes watching.

"How am I supposed to get to Mexico from here?" My voice sounds shaky, like maybe I *am* going to cry. Crying will be the end of me. I'm sure of it. If I cry, there will be no more *Emily*, no more *me* anymore. Emily doesn't cry. A fly buzzes close to my ear and I swat it away. I hope it doesn't look like I'm wiping my eye, because I'm not crying.

I am not.

Rex gets out of the car, but he doesn't go around and grab the gas pump. Maybe this is just some trick to get me out of his car. He cocks his thumb at a doorway off to the side of the Crossroads Bar and Grill.

Greyhound.

I feel the disappointment transform my face, but I

can't stop it. What did I think was going to happen? Was I so stupid to think we were going to have a big adventure together and be in love like some stupid movie? I wish I had a razor so I could make a cut big enough to make this stupid feeling go away. A cut that would bleed and bleed until everything was out of me.

He looks at me like I'm a child who doesn't understand the way the world works. The kid and the dog are staring too. Rex takes something out of his pocket, a dirty white business card. He looks at it, traces the raised letters with his thumb, then puts it away.

Fuck you, *Rex*, if that's even your name.

Fuck you.

"You wanna get something to eat before you go?" He walks around to the back of the car and pops the trunk.

The last thing I am is hungry, but there's this desperate feeling inside me and I don't care if I'm pathetic. I feel like once he drives away I'm going to be traveling alone through the land of the dead they talk about in fairy tales, or is that in myths? I feel the dread mounting like a wave. I've got one foot in the strange land. I'm a minute away from drowning in emptiness.

"Don't be scared," he says as he tucks a long, thin case under his arm and slams the trunk shut.

"I'm not scared of anything," I say.

But I am.

Barstow

Two thousand years ago, the 41.4 square miles of the western Mojave Desert that came to be known as Barstow was occupied by Indian tribes who lived beside the immense lakes that covered most of the Mojave.

In the late 1800s, Barstow became a mining center when borax was discovered.

By the 1960s, three major interstate highways intersected Barstow, and sewer and water services were extended to include the whole city.

By 2006 Barstow had a Home Depot.

FOUR

The Crossroads Bar and Grill is way more bar than grill. It's got neon beer lights and dark paneled walls and it smells like cigars and old beer.

Hank Williams Sr. or Jr. or whichever is the good one is singing: *Why can't I free your doubtful mind and melt your cold, cold heart.*

When Joey and I used to hang out at that karaoke place in the Village, I used to sing this song. It was his favorite. We slept in the fucking park because I couldn't find a job and Joey couldn't work, but we had some good times there. Those nights felt almost like when we were kids again, back before all the bad shit happened.

The Crossroads would look like any other downtrodden country bar, except it's got a big front window that looks out on the gas pump and a little front counter for selling cigarettes and pine-tree-shaped air fresheners and stuff you would buy at a gas station. Because of the window, the light is all wrong inside the bar. Rusty sunlight filters in through the dirty glass and makes it feel like some weird sort of brown twilight is falling.

The place is okay, I guess. Nobody says anything about me not having any shoes. Other than the bartender, a wiry old dude with long gray hair who looks like he knows his way around a meth lab, there's only one other guy in the place. He's a tall black guy with Jeri curls wearing a leather car-coat in spite of the fact that he's in the middle of the desert. He's shooting pool by himself.

Rex winks at me and holds his hand up like I shouldn't follow him.

Whatever.

I watch as he turns on his high-beam grin and saunters over to the guy at the pool table. They say something I can't hear, then shake hands. I am bored by the time Rex assembles his pool cue and go and sit at the bar.

"What can I get you, young lady?" The bartender looks like he's sizing me up. I worry that he's going to ask for my ID. But he doesn't.

"I'll have a tequila sunrise." I don't really drink anymore, even though I am—*was*—a cocktail waitress, but I always wanted to order one of those. They look really pretty. And it seems like the kind of thing you should drink in the desert when you're on your way to Mexico.

On the bar there's a plastic box containing slices of orange and lime and maraschino cherries. They look like they've been in that dish for weeks. A couple of flies swoop and dive into the gooey-looking syrup. I really hope a tequila sunrise doesn't need any fruit.

Before my drink hits the coaster, Rex is sitting next to me at the bar.

"I'll take a draw. Whatever you got on tap," he says as he hooks the heels of his boots on the rungs of the stool.

I swivel around to look at him. "I thought you were playing pool." Some of the cocky seems to have leaked out of him, but he still taps his foot to the music. It seems like he's forcing it.

"I did."

"That was fast."

"Lost."

"Did you only play—"

"Look, Kitty, I lost, okay. The whole wad. All or nothing. That's the game I play."

The bartender puts a beer in front of Rex.

"Can we get some eat?" Rex asks.

The bartender looks at his watch. "Burgers and chips only. No fries."

"All right. Two of each."

The guy takes a stub of a pencil from behind his ear and scribbles on a little curled-up notepad. He points his pencil at my drink, then at Rex's beer, and scribbles again. "Seventeen fifty." He looks at Rex.

"Hey, Kitty, would you mind?" He flashes his bright white smile at me. "You know how it goes. You win some, you lose some. It'll be all right. I've got a job starts tomorrow."

What the fuck do I care whether this dickhead is going to be financially solvent in the long run? I'm the one with the problem. I don't need this nickel-and-dime shit. "You want *me* to pay for this?"

He winks.

Fucking hell.

I twirl around on the chair so no one can see and raise up my shirt. I readjust the bungee cord because it's seriously not working like a belt is supposed to. I unzip the little pouch I wear around my waist and take out the credit card. JUDITH FORD. Ugh, I am so not a Judith. I rearrange everything so nothing looks bulgy and twirl back around and hold out the card. I think about whether I'd be pushing my luck to ask for a cash advance. I don't ask. There's got to be an ATM somewhere in this town.

The bartender takes the credit card and walks off into the back to do whatever and I think of whispering to Rex that he should call me Judith. I don't because he'll probably still call me Kitty anyway.

"What job do you have in L.A.?" I ask to cover up the sounds of Johnny Cash coming over the speakers singing: *We're in the jailhouse now...* I do not appreciate the universe fucking with me like that.

He puts his hand in his pocket and pulls out a business card, probably the same one he looked at outside. He shoves it in my hand.

The card has worn edges and is gray where it's been creased. JACK LORD. I read it and that name sounds like somebody I should know but I can't place it.

"That's right." Rex grins like he's just guessed the number of jelly beans in a jar. "Jack Lord. Detective Steve McGarrett. Whoo! Whoo!"

The guy at the pool table shakes his head like Rex is an idiot or a drunk or something.

"I was in Tipper's up in Truman. That's just outside Memphis and I was winning at pool like I *usually* do." He raises his eyebrow for emphasis. "And there sat Jack Lord Mr. *Hawaii 5-0* himself. So I walked up and introduced myself and one thing leads to another and we're having a good old time. And then he gives me that card and says if I'm ever in L.A., I should stop by and say hey. It was a sign. Like a gift from the Lord. Get it? The *Lord* sent me a sign."

I'm still not quite sure who Jack Lord is but I say, "Cool," and hand the card back. "But what's your job in L.A.?" I ask again, because I am pretty sure he didn't answer the question even though he acts like he did.

"I'm an actor. Actors gotta act." He grins his crooked grin and reaches in his pocket and pulls out his keys. He balances the gold charm on the bar and rubs its head.

It's a fucking Oscar statuette, I realize. "You've got a part in a movie or something?"

I'd buy that. He looks like he stepped out of some 1950's period piece about greasers. And of course he has those white teeth. He would be more movie-star handsome without the scar over his eye and the crooked nose, but not everyone gets to be the leading man.

"Relationships, Kitty. It's all about relationships." A flicker of annoyance flashes across Rex's face. "Jack Lord said to look him up when I came to town. That's like money in the bank."

"That's it?"

"What?"

"Based on that little interaction, you packed up and took off for L.A.?"

"Yeah."

"Holy fucking Christ, seriously?"

He must be joking, but I can see by the earnest look on his face that he is not. Fucking tragedy, if ever there was one.

"I'd like it better if you didn't cuss like that. The Lord don't like for folks to take his name in vain."

"What?" I take a sip of my tequila sunrise. It tastes just like gasoline mixed with orange juice. "All right, sorry. No *cussing*. But that is about the stupidest, most ill-conceived plan I've ever heard in my life. Do you even have a place to stay? A plan B in case this acting gig doesn't pan out? Tell me you've got money. Oh wait no. You just lost it all. Seems like you ought to be the one cussing."

Rex looks at me like I just kicked his puppy.

I roll the edge of a cocktail napkin around a little red stir stick so I don't have to look at him. Maybe I was kind of harsh. But the truth hurts. That is one fucked-up pre-teen-girl plan he's got going on. If he wasn't a dude and kind of on the old side, he'd end up on the streets giving blow jobs for crack money.

I look toward the door that the bartender disappeared through. What's taking so long?

"You know what your problem is, Kitty? You're afraid to dream. That's why you're all choked up inside and it spills out angry."

Heat rises up in me. I can feel my cheeks getting red. "That is total bullshit." I cover my mouth like I'm panto-miming and let it fall away so he knows he can't tell me what the fuck to say. "I've got a dream. But more importantly, I've got a plan. The plan is the thing. If you don't have one, you go off half-cocked and end up in jail or something."

I know this is true. Before I came up with the plan to get my ass to Vegas and find a decent singing gig, I was dangerously close to being in that situation myself. No way am I going to jail. And I sure as hell am not going to pick the option Joey chose. In New York they only know me as *female accomplice*. They don't even have a description. In Vegas no one has a clue. Going to Vegas was a great plan.

Until it wasn't.

Fuck.

I toss the straw and napkin at the trash can behind the bar. I miss. A whole bunch of flies swarm up into the brown hazy fake twilight air of the bar. I can't hear them buzz but I feel it inside my head like a vibration.

I don't know what I'm talking about, I'm taking the short bus to Mexico and I don't even have any shoes. If ever two losers are in the same boat, it's us.

Rex unhooks his heels from his stool and puts his feet on the floor like he's going to leave.

"Those burgers are taking a long time, aren't they?" I put my hand on his arm. I don't know why. I don't want him to go, I guess.

"You in a hurry?" he asks.

I shake my head.

"I know it's stupid, taking off like that," he says real low, almost a whisper. "But there's not all that much to stick around Truman for. There's nothing there. No work, no interesting people, nothing. Then my mom died and her house seemed real big and real small at the same time and it was filled up with the half-finished needlepoint and five different flavors of tea in the cabinet and every time the doorbell rang..." Rex looks over. "Do you believe in ghosts?"

"Of course," I say because saying no means I'm not going to hear the ghost story.

"Every time the doorbell rang, which wasn't so much, I could swear I'd hear footsteps on the way to answer it."

He stopped speaking like he was done.

"And?"

"And what?"

"What happened then?"

Rex contorts his face into a shape that says he is pondering the question. Maybe he really is an actor, because this expression of his is definitely playing to the back row.

"I'd go answer the door and it was the UPS fella with a package for my mom or something."

"That is about the lamest ghost story I've ever heard."

"It's not supposed to be a scary ghost story. I was explaining why I left. That was the reason. It was too sad to stay in that house with my mom still there but not really there. Just the wisps of her like dust on the floor that I should sweep away."

That's sweet, I guess, if sweet is the kind of thing you're into. The guy loves his mom.

"Seemed like the time was right. If I was ever going to do anything, you know *be* anything, I should do it then. And then the same week I had the idea to go, I met up with Jack Lord. It was a sign."

When he says it like that, it doesn't sound like the stupidest plan anymore. I sit for a second and try to imagine him in that empty house and it seems like he might be someone who understands that feeling of drowning in emptiness. I feel like I want to put my arms around Rex and hold on to him as tight as I can.

But I don't.

The bartender comes through the door without our burgers. He has a look on his face like someone's got a good grip on his balls. "Judith Ford?" he says with a businesslike tone that doesn't at all fit with ambiance of the establishment.

I hesitate a second too long, I guess.

He holds up the credit card and cuts it in two with some rusty scissors. "Keep your seat. I'm going to have to call the police."

Fuck! Fuck! Fuck!

I jump off the stool. It hits the floor with a crash. The gun catches on the bungee cord belt where I'd stashed it. The cord snaps when I tug it out. The magazine is loose. I pound it into the handle like I've seen on TV. A flow like undertow I can't control moves my arm.

Whatever's going to happen is going to happen.

The panic and fear and excitement are there but separate, like the wave has already crested. I pull the trigger. The shock jolts through me. I pull again. Again.

The bartender's face explodes. Blood and bits of stuff splatter the mirror behind him. There's a hole where his eye used to be. I watch him crumble and fall. He tips over the trash can.

The flies go wild.

"What'd you do?" Rex yells at me. He backs away from me like he's just seen a monster.

"He was going to call the cops," I yell.

Fuck! Fuck! Fuck!

What now? I've got to get out of here—fast.

"Come on, Kitty, we're friends. Don't shoot." Rex holds up his hands and smiles his gleaming white smile.

"I'm not going to shoot you with your own gun, stupid."

Unless you wink at me, then I will fucking kill you.

"That's my gun?"

"Yes," I say.

Rex is looking a little peaked like he's about to spew on his shoes.

"And now we're going to get the fuck out of here together,

because nobody's going to believe I did this by myself."

"Kitty, I gotta get to L.A."

"Fuck L.A.! That's a stupid plan."

Rex snaps his mouth shut.

"We need gas! We need money," I yell at him because he's not seeing the bigger picture.

Fuck!

I spin around and the pool player is edging his way to the back door. He raises his hands. Sweat is trickling down his neck into the collar of his coat.

"Give his money back," I yell. It comes out sounding way more shrill and crazy than I intend.

"Yeah, okay awright." He reaches into his breast pocket and throws a wad of cash on the pool table. "Here you go." He looks me in the eye like he's going to find my code of honor there.

I pull the trigger. Pull again. I can't hear anything but vibration between my ears.

The top of his head disappears. He crumbles to the floor.

"Turn the motherfucking gas on!" I scream at Rex as I snatch the money from the table and run for the door.

FIVE

The weird brown twilight of the Crossroads Bar and Grill follows us, merging with the cloud of dust and pebbles, churning up as we tear out of the parking lot.

"Go faster," I yell, even though we're going fast enough for the tires to slide on the road.

Fuck Fuck Fuck!

The nose of the car points up onto the highway. "No!" I scream. I grab the wheel and yank it.

The car veers.

Rex makes a howling sound like a kicked dog.

"Not the highway!" I yell.

The car bumps over the edge of the on-ramp and bottoms out hard enough for my teeth to slam together.

Rex probably meant to hit the brake but he hits the gas. The engine roars. The back end fishtails. Gravel and desert sand sprays behind us sounding like rain as the particles hit the car. We fly away from the highway at a perpendicular angle.

"Is this south? Is this the right way?" My voice sounds shrill and thin.

Rex doesn't say anything. He probably doesn't know either. At least we're on back roads and going faster than I've ever gone before. I can feel the fear inside me, but it's tucked away and separate. I know it could get out any minute and make me ache with it. But for right now, it's stashed away.

In no time at all, we're away from Barstow. For miles

and miles there is nothing to see but sand and Joshua trees and sometimes, a rock formation that looks like shadow puppets, hands in the shape of a jackrabbit. "Are you okay?" I ask Rex.

He doesn't say anything. He grips the steering wheel tighter and leans down close to it. He's grinding his teeth. His jaw twitches in that angry way men's jaws move when they're holding violence in.

The sun through the weird brownish haze is dropping closer and closer to the horizon. The glare on the road is fierce. I feel around on the seat for the sunglasses, but I can't find them.

I squint through the amber light into the setting sun's molten white core. A shadow—a silhouette—a person! "Stop!" I shriek. "Someone's in the road."

"Wha—" Rex starts to ask and then he sees the figure too. He slams his foot on the brake. We slide sideways, then spin. I hold on to whatever I can grab. The dashboard— the edge of the seat—air.

The Joshua trees wave their twisted arms as we spin past them, by them, through them.

And then we are tipping. My hands are wrenched free and I'm thrown into Rex. The gear shift bashes my knee. Rex's head slams into the steering wheel. For a moment, in spite of the pain in my leg, it feels thrilling like a roller coaster. Then I realize that ten tons of classic car are about to come crashing down on us. Miraculously my fear stays tucked away. And equally miraculous, the car stops moving.

Just stops.

I breathe out slowly, afraid to move in case the slightest vibration might cause the inertia to pick up where it left off. I'm on top of Rex with my face pressed into his neck. This is the first time I've ever touched him, I realize. His face is pressed against the side window. Blood drips from his eyebrow onto the glass.

I give it a moment to make sure it's really over. My heartbeat is slamming in my ears like a heavy metal anthem.

"Kitty," Rex says. It's not a question or even a statement. It's like the *amen* at the end of a prayer.

"Are you okay?" I ask as I contort myself into some backward then forward spider-walk and use my jungle-gym skills to get first off Rex, then out of the car. A twinge of pain shoots through me when I put weight on my leg, but it's not more than I can stand.

I am in the sea of wild landscape that flew by the car windows what seems like a lifetime ago. The road is barely a road. It's more like furrows in the ground just big enough to hold the tires. It's a child's road made in a sandbox with matchbox cars. This doesn't feel secure or even real. Who knew that blacktop and street signs could be a comfort? I'll bet this place isn't on any map.

Creaks, croaks and hums swirl around me as nocturnal beasts come alive. I think the thing that slithered away and hid under the car was a lizard. I hope it was a lizard. The desert is not as empty as it appears.

Once I'm on the ground, Rex has no trouble sliding out. His movements are stiff as he stands up. Maybe he is older than I thought.

"You're bleeding." I wrap the too-long sleeves of my shirt, his shirt, around my hand and reach up to wipe off the blood.

He shoves my hand away like he's mad or he thinks this is *my* fault. "Poor old Linda, she's the one that's hurt." He puts his hand on the passenger-side door that's up in the air. He's got a strange heartbroken look on his face. "I'm sorry, baby. We'll get you all fixed up."

"You can patch her up, Rex. She'll be as good as new," I say, because what the hell, the guy loves his car.

He spins around and glares in the direction we were going before we wrecked.

The sun sinks down below the horizon. It's not dark yet, but dark is coming fast.

I hate the dark.

In the golden-brown twilight up on a little ridge where two roads cross, stands the little black boy and the dog from back at the bar and grill. From back at the parking garage in Vegas?

Maybe now is the time I should do the math. This kid can't travel at the speed of light. Something is wrong here. Or maybe something is wrong with me.

I was never very good at math.

I can't see the looks on their faces but I can tell they're looking our way. Looking and standing perfectly still.

They must have wanted to come with us, I think, because my brain's kind of rattled from rolling around in the car. They followed us. I get that feeling like something is off again, but I don't want to examine it too closely. I don't want to turn over that rock. Something truly horrible might be under it.

Rex squares his shoulders like he's going to fight and stomps through the scrub and sand and broken cactus. "Hey!" he yells at them.

I run to catch up with him.

They don't flinch or respond in any way. Not the boy. Not even the dog. They remind me of a movie poster they're posed so perfectly against the dying blaze of the sun.

"You got no sense?" Rex yells as he breaks into a run. When he gets to the place where the two roads cross, he grabs the boy by the arm and yanks him. The dog snarls, but Rex doesn't pay any attention. "You're going to get killed standing in the road like that." Rex shakes the boy.

The dog bares its teeth and growls but it doesn't attack.

I rush up to Rex and put my hands on his arm to make him stop shaking the kid. "He didn't mean it. Did you?"

The little boy is making sounds like he's crying, but no

tears are coming from his big brown eyes. A fly lands on the corner of his mouth. The hum of it is too loud for a single insect.

Rex lets go of him.

And without even thinking about it like it's an instinct, I hug the kid and hold him really tight. The fly drone hums in my ears. He's skinny. I can feel his bones against me. His hair is wild and matted in dreadlocks like maybe his mother is white and doesn't know how to care for it. Or maybe she's dead a long time like my Chinese mother. His hair smells like the desert, dusty and dry. I get the feeling like we both know what it feels like to be drifting unmoored in the big emptiness. I rock back and forth with him. He stops making the crying sound.

A sound, a howl, rises up into the air. It's close by, no, far away. I can't tell. I don't know where the animal that is making this hollow, hungry sound is. The dog inches closer to the boy as if to protect him. Perhaps to step into the gravity of humans and away from the wild. The howl decays into yipping and whining.

Coyotes.

Must be, although it could as easily have been demons. The first howl is joined by another, another. A pack of coyotes.

I kept a rabbit in a hutch in my backyard when I was little. His name was Frank. I kind of had a dark side as a kid. He was awesome. He thumped at me when I didn't pet him enough. He nuzzled under my chin. His fur was the softest thing I've ever touched. Someone left the cage unlatched, and the cat got in his hutch.

Bunnies scream when they're scared. Scream like children who've been really hurt bad. Frank screamed when the cat got him. I couldn't get outside in time.

I might have been the one who left the hutch unlatched.

I did.

I left the hutch unlatched.

The pack of coyotes have captured something.

A rabbit.

The scream stabs me in the hole where my heart used to be.

Rex stomps back to his car shaking his head. He studies Linda as he walks around her. I can see his mouth moving like he's talking to her or maybe singing her a lullaby.

I let go of the boy and hold him away from me so I can see him better. He's got big brown eyes and an ordinary, cute kid face. He reminds me of someone the way he's looking at me. "What are you doing out here?" I ask.

And then I know. The thought hits me like a punch in the stomach. I ride the wave of hurt and panic until I can breathe again. He's looking at me exactly like the guy at the Crossroads Bar and Grill did. The guy playing pool. "That was your dad?" I ask even though I don't need to. "At the bar playing pool?"

He moves his head up and down. Not with enthusiasm or grief or any other sort of emotion I recognize. He just moves his head up and down like its bobbing on a wave.

I feel like I'm sinking. I feel like I'm going under.

The dog whines and paws at the ground by my naked feet.

The bunny is quiet now. The coyotes have moved on.

The boy is my responsibility. He's mine to care for. I'm taking him with me.

Whomp! The sound crashes through the desert silence. I flinch as if I've just heard the sound of the ax that's coming to lop off my head.

But I haven't.

Rex has pushed the car back into position. From my vantage point it looks the same as it always did except for a flat tire.

I scoop up the boy and run to the car. The dog trots along beside.

⁷¹ PONTIAC GTO

The Pontiac GTO is an American muscle car classic built by the Pontiac Division of General Motors from 1964 to 1974.

The 1971 GTO has wire-mesh grilles, horizontal bumper bars on either side of the grille opening and more closely spaced headlamps than previous models. The overall length of the vehicle is 203.3 inches. A GM corporate edict aimed at preparing the company for the soon-to-be-passed ban on leaded gasoline forced manufacturers to reduce the engine compression ratios. The top-of-the-line GTO engine in 1971 was the 455 HO with 8.4:1 compression. It had the power of 310 horses. With the optional 12 bolt posi-traction rear end and the 3.90 axle, it could go from 0 to 60 in 6.1 seconds and reach 102 mph in 13.4.

Only 357 GTOs were sold before the model was discontinued in February of 1971. Seventeen of these were convertible.

SIX

Rex holds the steering wheel lightly, like he doesn't want to cause Linda any more pain. The car looks pretty scuffed up. The front is buckled on Rex's side right over the front tire. Cracks in the windshield spread, making tiny *zings* and *pops* as the glass fractures. Something is wrong inside the car. The noise, metal on metal, sounds painful as if Linda is suffering from mechanical arthritis. She's moving slower too. Rex looks worried. He pets her dash intermittently and makes a cooing, clucking *everything will be all right* sound in his throat.

Maybe everything will be all right. In the long run. In the distant yet unimagined future.

I have my doubts.

The car's headlights aren't as bright as I would like. Their cones of light barely pierce the darkness. There isn't a sliver of moonlight in the sky. The stars are beautiful, sprinkled over the velvet black void, but they don't light the way. I wish for a glimmer of electric light. A street lamp or anything that would signal there is still such a thing as civilization and it hasn't disappeared from the mortal plane. I'm not one hundred percent sure that civilization is what I need. I haven't been doing so well with civilization so far. But I hate the dark.

I really hate the dark.

The boy sits in the middle of the backseat. He's swimming in all that space. Rex's suitcase is pushed over to one side. The boy holds the framed picture of the old lady, Rex's mother, I guess. I told the boy to put it down about fifty times, but he didn't. Probably the kid misses his mom. Maybe I should bring him up front and hold him in my lap.

But I don't.

He clings to his dog's neck. By the unearthly green glow that emanates from the dashboard, I can see the dog's face. The beast seems as if he's holding in a smirk. The creature is entirely hairless, rubbery-looking—implausible.

Rex is watching the kid through the rearview mirror. "You have any kids, Kitty?"

"Me? No. Hell no."

Every stupid bitch I went to high school with seems to have one or two. Like they're obligated or something.

"Did you ever think about it? What it'd be like," Rex asks. He's still got his eyes glued to the mirror.

"I don't know. No. Maybe. Do you have any kids?"

Rex has a look on his face. It's intense, reflective, like he's got something he's sorry about. Or maybe it's just the weird light from the dash.

"What if you get a bad one?" I say. "Seems like that could ruin your life."

I've seen brats running around screaming. Their mothers look old even when they're young.

"Kids are like people, Kitty. Sometimes they're bad; sometimes they're good. Just like anyone."

I never thought about it like that.

"That could be even worse," I say. "What if you love your kid more than anything on earth? What if you fuck up? *Screw* up, sorry."

"Yeah. Having a kid, loving a kid, makes you a bigger target."

"Why do people do it? I get how it works and all. But what makes you go through with it instead of going for the abortion like it makes sense to do?"

"I don't know, Kitty. I don't know."

One good thing about the dark is that I could see

flashing police lights from miles away. Just as I let that thought settle in, I see two orbs reflected in my side mirror.

Fuck!

My heart hammers its way up into my throat and I take a deep breath.

"Rex! You see those lights?"

"Yep."

"You think it's the cops?"

"Maybe."

"If the police come, where are we supposed to hide?"

I should have thought about that.

Fuck!

"I guess we'll take that road when we come to it. We'll just let the Lord guide us for now," Rex says as he winks at me like he knows something I don't.

How can he be so fucking calm!

I don't want to turn around in my seat because that'll only look suspicious, but I do. The lights are gaining on us fast. I kneel in the seat and clutch the headrest like it'll save me from the hail of bullets that will surely come.

The little boy looks up at me like he's never seen me before.

"Don't worry," I say. "Stay down."

I can't tell by his face if he's worried, but he's got to be feeling something.

I listen for a siren. For the *thump, thump, thump* of helicopter blades. I swear that dog is holding in a laugh.

The lights are close, closer. They flash and I wet myself a little. I spin around and drop down in the seat. I grab the edge and hold on as tight as I can. I'm waiting for the ax to fall.

A single *whomp*.

I ride the panic wave. It rolls and rolls but doesn't crest.

Rex steers the car onto the shoulder.

Finally, at the exact moment when I am going to die,

the rising dread abates. Whatever's going to happen is going to happen. I touch my hair. It doesn't feel like it's turned white.

The car is still rolling. Rex isn't pulling to a stop.

Tink, tink, tink, tink. A sound like music from a child's piano fills up the black desert vacuum. The tinkling notes coalesce into a tune—"Turkey in the Straw." A little truck with pictures of ice cream in all its many forms pulls ahead of us and speeds away.

"Catch it!"

I want to reach my leg over and stomp on the gas.

But I don't.

"Catch it. We need ice cream." I glance over my shoulder at the little boy. This is the thing that should make him happy. This is the kind of thing a kid would like.

Miraculously, Rex does as I say. Linda creaks and groans as her metallic joints grind. He honks the horn. *Aye-oooh-ga.* It sounds like a joke.

"Do you want ice cream?" I ask the boy.

He lifts his head up. "Yes." His voice is too loud, too old, too filled with echo—something. Maybe he's not really a kid. Maybe he's a midget—an alien—a giant bug in a kid's body. I want to grab him and examine him.

But I don't.

That's crazy thinking.

It's been a crazy day.

The ice-cream truck slows and pulls to the side of the road. I jump out of the car and run up to the window. The road is still hot. It remembers the sun. I almost do too as I pull out my last fifteen dollars from the pouch around my waist and buy the tastiest stuff I can. A Drumstick, an Orange Creamsicle, a Rocket. A tiny tub of vanilla with a wooden spoon for the dog.

The music tinkles out from the horn on top of the truck and spills over me. A warm yellow glow lights the woman's face on the other side of the sliding window. She smiles like everything is just fine—normal—ordinary. For a moment I feel like I never grew up, like I never turned bad.

"Seventeen fifty," she says in exactly the same voice as the bartender back at the Crossroads Bar and Grill.

Same voice.

Same amount.

Fuck.

The moment is lost.

I give her fifteen dollars and push the little tub of vanilla for the dog back to her. She studies me for a moment, then lets me have it for free.

I say thank you even though that is so inadequate I almost cry. I want to say more so she will know how important that moment was, even though it was only a moment. I want to say she's an angel. That I wish the whole world could dance on the head of her pin.

But I don't.

The remembered sun soaks into me from the hot sand through the soles of my feet as I watch the ice-cream truck drive away. *Tink, tink ta tink tink, turkey in the straw.*

The music washes away as the red taillights fade into the distance.

I bring the ice cream back to the car. The boy takes his from me like I owe it to him.

"What do you say?" I ask, because kids need reminding, I guess.

"Thank you."

I wish I hadn't asked him. His deep, echoing voice makes the panic I've got tucked away seep into my blood just a little.

As I get in the car, I've got a feeling something's not right. Something bigger than the obvious wrongs, the stuff I'm responsible for. If I'm responsible for this boy, am I responsible for all the wrong he might ever do?

Rex doesn't say anything when I give him his ice cream. He takes it though.

What do you say?

I don't have the courage to ask that question again. He doesn't really owe me anyway. The opposite, maybe.

Rex starts up the car and we limp off down the road deeper into the velvet black night.

I wish the ice cream tasted better than it did. I guess once you passed a certain point, there's no going back. I'm not a kid anymore. All the kid pleasures are gone.

Fuck.

And this is all that's left.

"Don't be mad at me," I say to Rex. "You can go to L.A. some other time. Jack Lord will still be there."

Rex doesn't look over. He is quiet for so long I'm afraid I've pissed him off more.

"You can't mess with a sign from the Lord," he says. His voice is kind of shaky.

"Look, you just made up the deadline for yourself. Nobody, not even God, said you have to be in L.A. in the morning."

Rex waves his hand like he's swatting at something. "You can't mess with a sign from the Lord," he repeats a little louder and a little slower like I'm deaf or—Chinese. "The Lord gave you a second chance and you went and killed two more people. That ain't right."

"Oh."

What if he's right? What if the Lord is real and he's as pissed at me as everyone else is?

Fuck!

"You know I had to do it, right?"

The dog is making a snorting noise like he's laughing. He stops slurping to do it. I gave that fucking dog ice cream. What is so goddamned funny?

"I didn't have a choice."

"You know what you done was wrong. You've got the voice in your head telling you right from wrong just like everybody else."

"I guess." I feel the wave of fear and panic rising up around me. It picked now to come out of hiding. I do not have a voice in my head. I could really use one of those. I could use someone on my side.

"Hey, Rex, I'm sorry, okay."

Linda makes a whining sound and Rex strokes the dashboard with a gentle, barely there touch. I wonder if loving a car like he does makes you a bigger target too.

"I really truly am sorry. I never wanted to get you mixed up in this sh— I never did want you to have to suffer for what I did. I am sorry."

I feel tears well up in my eyes like I'm some little crybaby girl. I don't want to cry now, not at this late date. What if I never stop?

I didn't cry when Frank the bunny died. I didn't cry when I left school or about what happened to Joey and what he did about it—any of the shit that happened. I didn't even cry when Joey...I don't cry.

Rex holds his arm out like he wants to give me a hug.

I slide across the seat and he lowers his arm and wraps it around me.

"Sometimes the Lord gives you more chances than you deserve." Rex squeezes me a little. It gives me more comfort than anything I can ever remember. "Yep. I've had more than my share of chances. Maybe you will too."

"You've messed up before and gotten another chance?"

"I've messed up big, Kitty. There's something I should probably tell you about what happened in Truman, Missouri..." He says the name of the state in that peculiar way Southern people do. His voice trails off like maybe he's not so sure he wants to tell me.

"You didn't really meet that actor guy?" I ask. "When

you were playing pool."

"Nope, that part's the God's honest truth." He just stops talking like that is the end of it.

"Then what?"

"That gun you used back there at the Crossroads bar, it's not mine."

Yeah right, dude, and everyone in jail *is* innocent.

"I took it off a guy."

"Seriously? It's stolen?" I feel him bobbing his head up and down.

"Well, technically, I guess it is. It was in the glove box when I drove off with Linda."

"No fucking way. You stole this car?" I lift my head up and look at him. His face is stiff, stoic. He doesn't take his eyes off the road.

"Fellow that had her wasn't treating her right."

"So you just stole the car. That is... I don't have the words."

"The point of me telling you that was to let you know that the Lord gave me another chance. I'm here with you today and not in some jail. Maybe he's going to give you one more chance too."

I hope what he says is true. I hope more than anything that is true because the darkness doesn't seem so terrifying as I lay my head on Rex's chest and listen to the *thump thump* of his heart. He smells familiar like home would smell if I had one, but also like oil and metal and sweat. He doesn't seem to mind if I stay next to him, so I do. I can hear the boy in the back snoring softly.

I hope Rex is right and this chance we got works out. I hope somewhere inside of me is a person who won't fuck it up. I stare at the road as it threads endlessly through the desert. Each of my eyes see the road a little bit differently. The double images separate and rejoin in a disjointed dance.

"I'm ashamed to call you my daughter."

I blink away the double vision. I don't move. I'm paralyzed. On the hood sits a woman who looks a lot like Elaine Chao, the Secretary of Labor, except she's wearing a getup that's so traditional no Chinese woman would ever actually wear it. I wonder why the wind whipping past doesn't blow off her Chairman Mao rice paddy hat and pull the chopsticks out of her hair.

"I'm not your daughter," I say.

I think I say.

"I'm not anyone's daughter. You didn't care enough to bring me up yourself."

"You are no good." The woman on the hood of the car scowls. "You helped your sissy boyfriend kill that boy. And then you ran away from your punishment."

You don't even know how much that son-of-a-bitch deserved it. He deserved more. After all the shit he did to me. Where were you? Isn't a mother supposed to stop bad stuff from happening? I'm not your daughter.

Thunder rolls across the desert. Lightning illuminates the sky behind my mother, my imaginary Chinese mother. For an instant she looks like she is sitting in front of a paper screen painted like a stormy sky. "You think only of yourself," she says.

I think about the boy...and Rex too. I care about them.

A strange truth occurs to me. For the first time since Joey died, I care about someone. I did not think that would ever happen again.

"I'm going to take care of them like nobody ever took care of me."

"You are a killer now, that's how you take care of people." The woman's scowl deepens. "You destroy them. You are no daughter of mine."

She turns away. And keeps turning—and turning until she is spinning like a fairy-tale character. She spins until she swirls away into the desert. A mother tornado. I feel the vacuum of her in my insides.

"Would you look at that?" Rex says.

"What?" I ask. My voice sounds thick with sleep even though I'm pretty sure I've been awake the whole time.

"You see that twister?"

"I do."

"The world is a mysterious place," Rex says.

Thunder rumbles across the desert. Lightning flashes in the sky. It looks like a paper screen painted with a stormy scene. My Chinese mother is gone.

The lightning flash decays to nothing.

When will this darkness end?

I am scared of the dark.

I am.

THE MAYAN CALENDAR

The Maya were a Mesoamerican civilization prominent from 2000 BCE to CE 900. The ancient Maya were the only people to master written language in the pre-Columbian Americas. They also developed mathematical and astronomical systems.

In the twenty-first century, the Mayan civilization is no longer a political entity, although the Mayan people are minority populations in southern Mexico and the countries of northern Central America.

The Maya are perhaps most famous for their calendars. The Sacred Round or Tzolkin measures a 260-day year with 20 periods of 13 days. Once a cycle completes, it begins again. The Tzolkin is a handy way to keep track of birthdays, anniversaries and holidays.

The Long Count calendar uses astronomy to track the universal cycle. Each cycle is 2,880,000 days or approximately 7,800 years. The Mayans believed that the universe ends and begins again at the start of each universal cycle. The latest cycle began on the fourth of Ahaw in the eighth of Kumku. It ended December 21, 2012, give or take a year or two.

SEVEN

I open my eyes and I can feel the sun burning through the fabric of my jeans and toasting my thigh. I sit up with a start. Rex pulls his arm back and chuckles. "Good morning." His laugh sounds kind of like he's forcing it. Not much to laugh about, I remember, as I fully wake up.

Thunder rumbles in the distance, rolling over the desert like a bowling ball flung down an alley. I wait for the crash and the fall of pins.

It doesn't come.

There's a damp spot on Rex's chest where I drooled on him. He doesn't say anything about it.

"What time is it?" I look at the dash.

"Don't know." He looks up at the sky. "One o'clock or so I'd say."

"One o'clock in the afternoon!" I feel woozy like I've been drinking. But I haven't. I'm sure I haven't.

There are clouds gathering overhead but they don't block the sun. It doesn't rain in the desert as far as I know. Why bother with clouds?

"Did you know the Mayans had a calendar that was hundreds of times more sophisticated than ours," Rex asks with a look on his face like he's ready to tell me all about it.

"I *did* know that. I saw a documentary, maybe two. I'm a regular scholar on the topic."

I should have tried harder like my white parents said. I could have probably gone to college. I was good enough in music to get a scholarship to somewhere interesting.

Not that I needed one. My parents would have paid. I get a melancholy feeling at the thought even though I hated school when I was there. I could have probably made some different choices. Made something more of myself.

Rex's eyes look kind of weary. He reaches under the dashboard and wiggles a wire or something when the car makes a strange noise. "Did your documentaries tell you that they predicted the end of the world?"

"Yeah, they mentioned it."

I just woke up, dude. Give me a fucking break with the news updates.

I twist around and look in the backseat. The boy is stretched out with his head lying on the photo of the old lady. His mouth hangs open and a fly buzzes around his lips. It's joined by a second that skitters out of his mouth.

"Close your mouth, Harvey," I say. "Or the flies will get in."

Or out as the case may be. Kids are gross.

He doesn't move.

The dog is curled up beside him. It's completely hairless except for a tuft of white hair on the crown of its head. It is a seriously ugly beast. The boy looks sweaty and the sun's hitting him right in the face.

"We've got to put the top up," I say.

I feel sick like I slept through Christmas. When I was a kid, I didn't think the sun would come up if I wasn't awake to make it happen. I've never been much of a sleeper. And now when the darkness is worse than it's ever been, I've missed hours and hours of light.

"Top's not working," Rex says.

I am not taking very good care of the boy already. I look at his little back moving up and down under his dirty white T-shirt. He's breathing. At least he's not dead yet. I want to shake him a little to see him move. But I don't.

"I've got to feed him," I say.

Rex doesn't respond.

"Do we have water?"

I could use some myself and a shower and maybe a coffee from Starbucks.

Rex shakes his head and jiggles whatever he's jiggling under the dashboard. I notice some steam coming up where the windshield meets the hood. It could be a mirage, though. The desert is supposed to be rife with those. The car seems to be moving slower than it was before and now it's making a hissing sound.

Who the fuck drives through the desert without water? I remember it's my fault. I still can't quite shake the feeling of being pissed off at Rex.

I'm so thirsty it feels like the dreams I used to have when I drank. I'd drink glass after glass of water but it was never enough.

Could I walk back to civilization if I had to?

Without shoes?

The desert spreads out to the horizon. Not even a telephone pole breaks the wildness of it. The vista is more than immense. Walking from one end to the other isn't a difficult distance to travel. The journey is more than an obstacle to be overcome with determination and willpower, it's an impossible feat. Truly impossible, like flying bird-style or becoming invisible. The fact that I am already too far in to make it back under my own power is no joke.

This isn't like the time I accidentally ended up in Florida and had to hitchhike back. That was hard. This is impossible. No amount of putting one step in front of the other will get me out of this alive. Plus a kid and a dog—and Rex.

Like the executioner's ax, the big picture slams down on my head. I'm a helpless little meat bag wandering in a vast wilderness with no water, no food, no shelter and I've got a kid to keep alive. I will shrivel and die. Getting busted for multiple murders might have been the better option.

Rex pushes on the gas pedal and the car shimmies and shudders.

"What's wrong with the car?" I hear the panic seeping into my voice.

Rex leans close to the steering wheel. Linda groans and cries out in pain as he pushes her down the road, such as it is. "There's something up ahead."

I look but I don't see anything. He's probably got heat stroke. A headache is throbbing behind my eyes.

I squint and I can just make out some weird shapes. Like a Stonehenge monument, a circle of tiny buildings looms off in the distance about ten city blocks away. The buildings are the exact color of the desert as if they were built from the sand. If they really are buildings and not just some trick of the light.

Linda creaks and squeals like her mechanical arthritis is acting up. She limps on toward the mission. She might make it that far. Probably not.

The semicircle of buildings takes shape in the distance. I can't believe I didn't see them before. They're stucco with tile roofs. Not that fake kind of stucco that you see in every suburb, these buildings look authentic like the mud bricks were made by hand. The colors go with the landscape, but they don't make the buildings invisible. I know I looked in this direction before and didn't see them. I thought about asking Rex if that was the kind of thing God might do, but I didn't want to come off sounding crazy. What if it wasn't the kind of thing God would do?

"Did you know this was out here?" I ask. "Because it seems pretty weird that there'd be something up ahead at the exact moment the car breaks down. Pretty fucking convenient."

"Ask and ye shall receive." Rex pats the car. "Those are the Lord's very own words."

"Your Bible shit is starting to get on my nerves. You know that?"

Why can't he just be quiet for a minute? Is that too much to ask? I have not had any coffee.

Rex scoots up in his seat as though doing that will make the car go a little farther.

"Just because you don't believe it, doesn't make it not so." Rex smiles that particularly smug smile that believers have. "If it wasn't for God smiling down on me, I wouldn't even be here. I'm blessed."

"*Blessed* is that what you call this shit storm we're embroiled in? Blessed?"

Linda grinds to a halt a block or two away from the mission. Rex turns the key off and the car goes dead. Steam pours out of the grate at the front and wafts back to steam up the windshield. It smells like burning plastic and hot tar. He pulls out the keys and rubs the head of the little gold statue with his thumb.

Before Rex can open his mouth to piss me off more, the boy stirs in the backseat. The dog hops to attention and barks. The sound of it rolls across the desert to meet the thunder. Without any more fanfare, the weird naked creature from hell jumps out of the car and faces the odd buildings in the distance. He growls and snarls. If he'd had hackles, he would have raised them.

"Silence," the boy says in his too-deep-for-a-kid voice as he climbs up over the door and jumps down in the sand. "I don't want to go there." The kid points to the mission's front door.

If he's got a better idea, I'll damn sure listen to it. I don't much want to go there either.

The dog whines and Rex turns on it like he might grab something and smack it. "That's one ugly mutt, right there. What's his name?"

"Chauvey," the boy says.

"Whoo! Whoo! Not your name, Harvey, the mutt's name." Rex ruffles the boy's hair as he studies the dog for a minute. "I'm going to call him Baldy, what do you say?"

The boy shrugs.

He tilts his head like he's listening for something. "In the dry place I eat *ranas* for a hundred years. Nothing happens to me."

That's a weird thing to say. Do all kids spew random creepy bullshit?

"You ain't a hundred years old, kid." Rex chuckles but it's not very convincing.

"We should go." I take Harvey's hand and start walking toward the buildings. His hand feels weird and tiny in my hand like I'm holding a bird with hollow bones. If I'm not careful, I might squeeze too hard and break them.

The dog acts like he doesn't want to go, but he follows us anyway. I guess he doesn't want to be separated from Harvey.

"Hey, Kitty, you think Linda's going to be safe out here by herself?"

Rex could use a shave and he's got some shadows under his eyes from lack of sleep, but he still looks pretty good. I am probably a wreck. I don't even want to know. I try to think of something witty to say, but the concepts just won't coalesce. "She'll be fine, Rex. She'll be just fine."

The guy loves his car.

The dog whines as we walk. It annoys me more than it should. I fight the urge to grab a rock and throw it at him.

The kid is dragging his feet. This is going to take forever. I hope I don't have to carry him. I will, if I have to, but I hope I don't.

I hear a sound. It's separate from the rolling, faroff thunder, the dog whining, and the scrunch of our feet in the dusty sand. A *peep, peep* sound. "Do you hear that?" I say out loud because of course they do. As soon as the words leave my mouth, we're deluged with a choir of peeping.

"*Ranas*," Harvey says. He's got a half-smile on his face, a smirk. Do little kids smirk?

"*Ranas*," Rex says with a nod.

The sound is like a plastic imitation of an animal noise as if someone pulled a string on a giant toy. *This is what the frog says.*

"Are those frogs?"

"Yep, *ranas* is Spanish for *frogs*," Rex says with a superior tone.

"Aren't frogs aquatic?"

Rex thinks for a moment. "Yep, I believe they are."

Rex strides down the path. His step grows bouncier the closer we get.

I wait for him to make the connections. But he doesn't. Good thing he's attractive.

Amphibians don't live in the desert. But here we have irrefutable evidence of the existence of *ranas*—in the desert.

Why?

The peeping hits a crescendo and settles to a constant level.

A panicky feeling starts creeping over me. I squeeze Harvey's hand, but not too hard. "You like frogs, Harvey?"

"No." The boy jerks his hand away and turns to go back to the car.

Fuck.

I run after him and scoop him up.

"I don't want to go. It's bad for me there." He twines his arms around my neck and his legs around my waist. He smells kind of froggy, like maybe he had been eating *ranas* for a hundred years.

"It's going to be okay," I say, which may be a lie. "It's going to be okay." I rush to catch up to Rex again.

"You know, Kitty, couldn't hurt you none to learn a little Spanish, what with you on your way to Mexico and all."

"Couldn't hurt me *any*," I correct him.

"That's what I'm saying." Rex flashes his brilliant grin. "I could teach you. *Como se—*"

"No, you said *none*. The correct word is *any*. It wouldn't hurt you *any*. Seems to me you should learn to speak one language before you start on a second."

Rex looks at me like I ate his last Oreo.

I guess I was a little mean. I'm cranky. It's hot holding this kid.

A cloud passes in front of the sun. My heart flutters. For an instant it feels like night is falling. I look up. That is one hefty cloud over my head. Black and pregnant with moisture, it looms over me as if threatening to blot out the sun.

As we draw closer, it's obvious the buildings are a mission. The pocked adobe is crumbling in places. Vines weave in and out of a trellis that covers the front wall. The leaves, shaped like hearts, reach up and climb onto the tile roof. The mission even has a bell in a tower.

Charming.

Baldy the dog does not want to have anything to do with this place. He turns one way then the other and whines. Harvey squirms in my arms. If I let him go now, he'd run away and I'd never catch him. I'd like to put him down. But I don't.

A woman, wearing black nun's robes with a wide white collar, steps through the doorway. She looks too young to have a job as a nun. She waves like she knows us.

I doubt that's the case.

"Here we go," Rex says like he knew all along we were going to find a nun in the middle of nowhere. Like he's happy about it. Like it solves all his problems.

It's too hot for that uniform. I'll bet she's every bit as uncomfortable as I was in my stupid showgirl dress. Whoever decided that women's clothes should be all about suffering? We all have our burkas to bear, I guess. At least she gets reasonable shoes.

The nun grabs the rope hanging next to the door and pulls. The bell tolls. Thunder rumbles. The two sounds pass each other as one departs and the other rolls in. Thunder cracks like a gunshot right over our heads. Icy drops hit me and fall to the ground. They bounce.

Heavy balls of ice smash into the car. Even though it should be too far away to hear, I hear: *thump, thump, thud* as hailstones pummel Linda.

The ground turns white with ice. A sharp chunk pelts my shoulder. I cover Harvey's head and run for the door.

EIGHT

A door should be an entrance—or an exit, not something that is neither, nor a combination of the two. That's the way doors work. What's the point of having a fucking door if going through it only leads back outside?

Harvey clings to me as I run through the door straight into some kind of courtyard. It doesn't have a roof and the ground is covered in hailstones. The hail looks like a dusting of snow.

Pretty, the white against the pink blossoms of the roses and bougainvillea, but strange.

Confusing.

The nun scampers after me and grabs my arm. "This way." Her voice is nearly drowned out by the drumroll of the hail. She pulls me under a covered walkway but not before a huge hailstone nails me on the head. At least they put a roof on some damned thing.

Rex grins at me with his snow-white smile as if he knew all along how the place was laid out. I suppose he doesn't realize I'm suffering from a hammer blow to the head that does nothing to relieve the headache behind my eyes, or maybe he's an asshole. At least that rock didn't hit Harvey.

I set the boy down on the ground. He clings to my leg and holds on tight. The hail stops. The silence hangs in the air, heavy and threatening. I wait for a bomb to explode, which is ridiculous, I know, but that's how it feels.

No bomb explodes.

Like nothing ever happened, the sun reappears and glares down on the compound like it's just another day in the desert. The frosting on the ground curls up and disappears, leaving only the largest chunks to drip and sweat like pieces of old snowmen.

"I'm so excited you're here," the nun says.

The nun has chipmunk cheeks. A moon face, my white mother would call it, sprinkled with freckles. She's light-skinned, but something about the way she holds her mouth as though it's poised to speak Spanish signals that she isn't Caucasian. Tendrils of her hair bounce as if to emphasize her words. She doesn't wear one of those nun hats. My white mother would have been happier if I had turned out like this girl. She never said it, of course.

She didn't have to.

My mom never really got over the fact that I didn't go to college. That I did what *I* wanted instead of what *she* wanted. In retrospect, I'm thinking that maybe I could have toned things down a bit. Maybe when I get to Mexico, I'll give her a call and let her know she wasn't completely wrong.

"And you brought a little child," the nun says. "I love children. Children are a gift to us all. I am so very happy you're here. It feels like my birthday."

Take a breath already, damn.

She reaches out to Harvey.

He makes a startled sound and pulls back. He bares his little pebblelike teeth.

Baldy growls a warning and he too bares his teeth.

I hope I'm not going to have to deal with biting.

"We'll be good friends before you know it." She hugs herself to express her joy. She is so cheerful she is actually wiggling.

I'm wondering how hard I'd have to squeeze her head to make it pop.

"We had an accident a while back," Rex explains. "Poor ole Linda, that's what I call her, my car. You know what *linda* means in Spanish?"

The perky nun shakes her head.

I call bullshit. This chick is Mexican.

"Means *beautiful*." Rex looks like he could scoop her up and give her a hug. "And beautiful she is!" Rex is positively glowing. "'71 Pontiac GTO with eight horses, dual overhead cams, a posi-track rear end..."

He continues, but it all turns to *blah, blah, blah*.

The nun locks her sparkling, enthusiastic eyes onto his. Bitch.

"She's going to need some work to make her road worthy," Rex says. "I can do the body work once I get her to L.A., but she's not going anywhere without a patch to her radiator."

"Father can help you with that. He's very handy."

All the while they've been talking, the nun has been leading us along the walkway. We pass doors with metal straps holding the wide wooden slats in place. The doors look like they belong in an Old West fort. Howdy, Sheriff. Right nice weather we're having.

We pass one with its door ajar. Inside there's a tiny wooden bed and a roughhewn stand holding a ceramic pot. A chamber pot! What the fuck. The tiny room looks as though it should be behind glass in a museum, like letters from Buffalo Bill might be in the drawers of the writing desk.

A hunky-looking version of Jesus on the cross hangs crooked on the wall like some lonely little nun has hastily replaced it. *Fuck me, Jesus*, I can't stop myself from thinking. Chances are I'm going to hell anyway. If there is such a thing.

Harvey grips my hand and clutches my leg. It makes walking difficult, but I don't shake him off. I think about it though. Baldy slinks along with us. He growls at everything. The dog does not seem to like it here. The boy doesn't seem all that thrilled either. He's a weird kid. He's not interested in anything. He just keeps his eyes focused straight ahead.

"Are you the only one here?" I ask, because what the hell is she doing out here in the middle of nowhere. This place is seriously weird.

"Father and I are caretakers for the mission."

Something's not right but I can't say what it is. I've got this feeling that's making the hair on the back of my neck prickle.

Maybe they've got a phone. Or, I don't know, a telegraph machine. What's the Morse code for SOS? Ha! Save Our Souls. That's a good one.

"Where is your father?" I ask. He's probably not *her* father, I think, as soon as the words leave my mouth. But who knows, maybe he is.

Rex shoots me a look like I'm being rude.

I guess maybe I did use a little bit of tone. Freckles, the cheerful nun, doesn't seem to mind.

"Father's gone down to the well. He should be back before long. I'm sure he heard the bell. Are you hungry? I've prepared a meal. It's extra yummy." Freckles smiles and gestures to an open door.

A single fly, bigger than an ordinary housefly, zooms and swoops through the doorway.

The nun narrows her eyes and looks at Harvey as she reaches into the folds of her habit in the general area where a pocket might be and takes out something that looks like a rolled-up newspaper.

Fuck.

They get newspapers.

"Father always comes when he hears the bell." She gives me one of those looks mean girls give when teachers or their parents are around. Or maybe it's not that kind of look at all, but something about it makes me edgy.

She swats at a fly.

As soon as she swats one, there are more. They perch

on the doorjamb, the lips of the flower boxes and every surface they can find. The nun's swatting only stirs them up. They're bigger than any flies I've ever seen. I'll bet their maggots are seriously disgusting.

"Ouch!" Rex grabs his neck. "Damned biting flies." His face turns bright red. "Sorry, Sister. I didn't mean to cuss." He smacks his arm, his thigh, his shoulder.

The flies aren't biting me.

I look down at Harvey.

The nun laughs all delicate like. "Are you hungry?"

"I *am* hungry," Rex says and grins extra wide. He scratches the welt on his neck as he waits for me, Harvey and Baldy to pass through the door. I try to catch Rex's eye because what the fuck is wrong with this picture, but he's too busy making googly eyes at the little Lolita nun.

The room, just like the rest of the place, looks like it belongs in a museum. In the corner, a big cast-iron pot blips and glubs on a wood-burning stove. A long, rough-looking picnic table is set with five settings just like they knew we were coming.

They couldn't know we were coming.

"Is that a newspaper?" I ask.

Obviously.

"May I see it?"

The nun gives it to me still rolled up.

It's got a squashed fly stuck to it. I scrape it off and unroll the paper. The headlines are in some weird language I don't recognize, Cyrillic or Arabic or something. The numbers are the same though.

It's the 584th of Tzolkin. Or it would be that if that's how you pronounce a *Z* facing the wrong way. They must be using the Chinese calendar. I should have learned how that thing works. Is it the year of the Tzolkin? The name sounds like one of those animals they only have in Australia.

The pictures in the paper are blurry and grainy to the

point of being incomprehensible. At least they are to me.

"Thanks." I give the paper back to her. The good news is neither my name nor picture made the headlines.

There's always tomorrow.

"Please have a seat," the nun says. She's smiling like one of those pictures of saints on the candles at the grocery store. Her happiness is way out of proportion to reality.

I mean, I'm happy too, but damn. Okay, I'm relatively happy... All right, I could eat something.

Rex grabs Harvey and swings him up in the air before plopping him down on the bench.

The kid doesn't squeal or squirm or react at all. Is something wrong with him? Is he sick?

Rex sits down next to him, unfolds a napkin and puts it in Harvey's lap. The kid looks like he's scanning the place for an escape route.

Sister of the Blessed Good Cheer motions me to come over by her.

I go over by the stove and she puts a knife in my hand.

It does not look that sharp.

"Will you slice the bread?" she asks.

Why me? Is there something about having a uterus that predestines me for kitchen duty? I hate that sexist shit. I hate it most when it comes from women. But what the fuck, it's just a little bread.

"Sure," I say. "What's your name? Or...what should we call you?" I ask her mainly because I'm running out of nicknames to amuse myself with.

A round loaf with an X on the top sits on a stone plate. It looks more artisan than artisan. It looks authentic. With the knife, I saw on it. The blade could be sharper.

"I'm Sister Azrael."

Azrael, why does that name sound familiar? Isn't that the angel of something? Weird name for a nun.

"You hungry, kid?" Rex asks Harvey.

"I don't eat the food for the dead." He shoves the tin plate away.

The nun's mouth falls open and she stares at Harvey like he took a shit on the baby Jesus.

"Ha, ha." I make myself laugh. I don't think I'm fooling anyone. "Kids say the weirdest things."

I'm kind of wishing I was sitting next to Harvey instead of across from him because it'd be easier to ignore the defiant look on his face. Is he about to have a temper tantrum? I'm not sure what to do if that happens. At least he'd finally be doing a kid thing. I suppose I should smack him. I think that's what you're supposed to do.

Harvey, true to his word, doesn't touch the food on his plate.

Baldy doesn't have similar qualms. He slurps and gulps from the dish the nun gives him. It's the most disgusting noise I've ever heard.

Sister Azrael, Azzie I'm going to call her for short, doesn't eat anything herself. She sits down right next to Rex and slides a big leather-bound book in front of her. She opens it up. Flecks of dust rise up from it and glitter in the light streaming in through the window. Bet that old thing has a serious silverfish infestation. Wedged in between the parchment pages is a bird feather. She takes it out and dips it into a bottle of ink. These people take their reenactment fantasies way too seriously.

"Name of the Mister?" Azzie flutters her eyelashes at Rex.

He doesn't seem to mind one bit.

"You want to write my name in that book?"

"I do." She leans over and kisses him on the cheek.

I didn't think nuns were supposed to do shit like that.

Rex looks at her like he's in love or some fucking thing and tells her his name.

She writes it in big flourishy letters, then looks at me.

"Me?"

She nods.

"Emily," I say.

Fuck, I should have lied about my name. The last thing I need is to be on the record.

"Emily...Dickinson."

She doesn't react to the name even a little. She just writes it down and looks at it on the page. She picks up her napkin and leans across the table to dip the corner in my glass of water. She rubs the page like she's trying to wash one of the names away. I can't see which one.

A darkness blocks the light from the door.

"Fra Serra!" The nun squeals with glee. She snaps the book shut.

SPANISH MISSIONS

Fra Juníper Serra, on behalf of the royal family of Spain, founded the mission system California. He worked at the enterprise until his death at age 70.

The purpose of the missions was to convert and educate the Native Americans in the hopes of turning them into ordinary taxpaying citizens.

El Camino Real, The Royal Road, connected all of the California missions. It eventually became Highway 101.

After Mexico gained independence from Spain in 1821, it could no longer afford to keep the missions running. The land and buildings were offered for sale to the Native Americans. Still not in favor of making payments to invaders, they declined.

During his presidency, President Abraham Lincoln formally required the return of the missions to the Roman Catholic Church. The missions that haven't declined into an unsafe state of decay still operate as churches. They hold regular services.

Most are open to the public.

NINE

"Hey, Kitty." Rex rolls a cigarette and dampens it down with his lips before handing it to me. That kind of grosses me out, but I take it anyway. "You ever watch one of them telenovellas on the Spanish TV?"

"I've seen them, I guess, flipping through channels. But I've never watched one all the way through if that's what you mean. Why?"

He flicks open his Zippo and strikes it for me. I only ever smoked weed and I almost choke myself on the first hit of the cigarette.

We're sitting in chairs made of wood slats out in front of the room Sister Azzie says is going to be ours. The room is small and cramped as a cave with a bed that's only a little wider than a single and a cot for the kid. I guess they think we're married. They must, because they're religious and it doesn't seem like they'd approve of out-of-wedlock shenanigans. I sure as hell don't want to tell them the real story.

The sun's hovering around the horizon. The light is causing all the shadows to turn painterly shades of pink and violet. Dark will show up before long. I'm dreading the dark more than usual. I can't really say why. I've got this feeling like sleeping in that little bed is the point of no return. Stupid, I know. I passed that bump in the road a long time ago.

"I've been thinking I might have a face that'd be good for Spanish TV," Rex says.

The magic-hour light is especially kind to Rex. He isn't

bad. Not at all. I'd hook up with him under normal circumstances, but circumstances aren't all that normal.

"Yeah, I can see that." I smile at him. I don't think I've smiled once through this whole thing. It feels good.

"I'm going to look into that once we get to Mexico." Rex scratches his leg with his thumbnail. Then he scratches his neck. That fly bite looks like it's getting infected. It's swelling up.

That's pretty awesome that Rex is planning what to do in Mexico. It's like we're together in this for real.

Cool.

It feels like we're at a motel, like we're on some family vacation. The stuff that happened—Vegas, Barstow—seems like a long time ago. Like it happened to somebody else. I get this feeling like we're in Mexico already.

Safe.

The outline of *The Padre,* as Rex insists on calling him, materializes at the distant edge of the mission compound. He's got Harvey sitting up on his shoulders, which is seriously weird considering how hard Harvey fought when the father first suggested he show Harvey the well. I like the idea that someone else would be in charge of the kid for a minute so I pulled him off me and handed him over. That kid can really scream. I'm not sure why he would need to see a well, but whatever. Maybe the father secretly baptized him. Couldn't hurt, I guess. The kid seems like he's going to grow up to be a troublemaker.

Baldy lopes along beside the boy and the priest. Their shapes are silhouettes that gradually take on dimension. At least he's bringing Harvey back. All priests can't be bad, right?

I'm not sure what this feeling is I have. It's kind of like having a two-beer buzz when a band is playing a really great song. I wish we could all stay frozen in this old-postcard moment forever.

The padre, Harvey and the dog get close enough for the twilight to light up their features. The jowly good-natured face of the priest looks kind and peaceful...or whatever that look is that religious people wear on their face. He looks like an ideal priest. A statue.

Harvey does not look happy. He's wearing a scowl that would put my old boss Mort to shame. His fingers are knotted in the father's hair. That's got to hurt. Baldy is watchful and wary, as tense as a cat.

The father swings the boy down from his shoulders and plants him on the ground. Harvey runs full out toward me and Rex. He holds out his arms and leaps into my arms. "Kitty. Don't ever make me go with him again."

His voice is different. It doesn't sound so grown-up anymore. It sounds like he's been auto-tuned up into the kid register. Kitty! What the fuck? I open my mouth to correct him but I don't. What the hell is he supposed to call me? I think through the obvious possibilities, my name for example. Do I really want a kid yelling out my name at all the wrong times? Kitty's the best of the bunch. It will have to do.

"What happened? Did he hurt you?"

I'm thinking of every story I've ever heard about priests and kids. Shit. I hope I didn't fuck up already.

The weird naked dog jumps up on Rex and licks his face. I will never get used to that dog. Rex doesn't seem to mind. He tousles its rubbery head and chuckles.

"Nothing happened. No one was injured. Isn't that right, son." The father is breathing kind of heavy, loud enough to hear, and he's sagging like he's worn out. He *is* a pretty old guy.

Harvey grins. It's a malevolent twisted thing that doesn't belong on the face of a child. "That is correct. The priest could do nothing to me."

Rex gets up and gives the father his seat. This saves me

from having to do it. I'm glad I'm not a dude.

The father drops into Rex's chair with an old-man grunt. "Run along and play fetch with your dog." The father throws a baseball across the courtyard to where Sister Azzie is piling up bundles of sticks in a heap like she's planning to make a gigantic bonfire. "Let the grown-ups talk."

I didn't even see the ball in the priest's hand. It was like it just materialized when he needed it. Priests don't have that power, do they?

"That's a good lesson for the boy to learn," Rex says like he's been thinking about the kind of things Harvey needs. Maybe he is going to stay with us. That would be pretty awesome.

Baldy and Harvey sprint after the ball.

"What's the story with the child?" the father asks once Harvey is out of earshot.

My heart leaps up into my throat. I glance at Rex but he's watching Harvey and Baldy and pretending he didn't hear the question. That's some bullshit.

"No story." I shrug like I'm calm, not worried, not scared.

Across the compound in the opposite direction from where Rex is *still* looking, Sister Azzie pulls on a rope and erects a pole in the center of the wood. Faggots. The word pops into my head. That's what they used to call wood like that back when they burned witches at the stake. And if all those woodblock prints I used to pore over in junior high were accurate, that's exactly what Sister Azzie is erecting.

That's crazy though.

Sister Azzie winds her rope around some sort of stake in the ground. Some sort of *permanent* stake in the ground, like they erected poles and build pyres often enough that they had permanent fixtures that helped make the work easier.

Fuck.

But that's just my imagination running away with me.

Seriously.

I laugh to myself. These perfectly nice people aren't going to burn a witch at the stake. There probably isn't a witch for miles, or a heretic or…infidel.

"He's not yours though." The father gazes at me with that damned beatific smile of his. He looks more like a statue than a human being.

Fuck.

I'm completely going to have to lie to a priest. Oh well, what's the worst that could happen? I glance at Sister Azzie. She has a rag wrapped around the end of her stick. She's pouring some sort of liquid on it. It bursts into flames.

"That's an odd thing to say," I say, because I can't say *None of your fucking business, asshole* to a priest. "Rex, honey. Did you hear what the father said?"

I have never in my life called anyone *honey*. The word sounds flat, like I'm reading it from a script. No one is fooled.

Rex looks away from Harvey and Baldy and gives me a crooked grin. "Yep."

The old father's face morphs into something that isn't quite so saintly. The flames from the pyre reflect on his glasses. He's seriously creeping me out.

The priest folds his hands and looks over at Harvey and Baldy. They are romping and running in circles around the fire. Something about the way they're moving makes me think of actors pretending to be children at play.

"Be careful," I yell. I get up from my chair and stand beside Rex. I could really use some moral support from him, but he doesn't seem to have any to give. I ought to go get Harvey and keep him close to me. It's dark now. We should go to bed. Although I can tell already that I'm not going to be doing any sleeping. How could that good feeling I was having crumble to shit so fast?

I grab Rex's hand and squeeze it tight. I like that I'm

blocking the priest's view of the boy. My boy. Our boy.

"I'd like you to consider leaving him here with us. That would be the best thing for everyone."

"No fucking way!" I say.

Rex tightens his grip on my hand. It hurts a little.

I don't care if the old man is a priest.

No fucking way.

I let go of Rex and spin around. "Harvey! Harvey, come over here right now." My voice quavers and doesn't sound authoritative at all.

Harvey stops running and jumping. The fire roars behind him. Sister Azzie puts a hand on his shoulder.

I have this feeling like they're planning to throw all of us on their bonfire. What if they're cannibals living way out here all alone? We'd probably keep them in picnic fare for months.

That's the crazy at work, I tell myself, and shake the idea from my head. Things are a little weird. They aren't full-on horror-movie weird.

Don't touch him, he's mine. You can't take him from me.

"Harvey! Now!"

Harvey runs toward me. Baldy scampers along beside him.

Sister Azzie follows him. She's carrying her rag-wrapped stick like Joan of Arc or The Statue of Liberty, I guess, because Joan of Arc didn't really get to be in charge of the torch. Something about the way she looks makes me think of Joan of Arc. The expression on the sister's face looks like she's on a righteous mission. The look in her eyes frightens me.

Harvey plows into me and throws his arms around my knees.

"I don't want to have to get the authorities involved." The father stands up. The kindly expression flickers across his face, even though kindly is the last fucking thing he is. No one is taking Harvey away from me.

No one.

"What authorities," I yell at him. "What the hell are you talking about?"

With movements faster than an old man should be able to make, he lurches toward me and grabs Harvey. He lifts the boy's shirt.

Welts, ugly purple raised ridges, striate his back.

"What happened, Harvey?" I'm having trouble catching my breath. Is it even possible to prove a negative? I didn't do this to Harvey. Is that what the priest is saying? Is he implying that I'd abuse a child? "Who did that to you?"

Harvey doesn't say a word. He struggles and claws to get away from the old man.

I am not in any way responsible for any harm done to this child. I'm protecting him.

"Rex, tell him I'd never do something like that. I'd never hurt anyone."

"That's the...truth," Rex says in his folksy way. But he's acting. It's on his face that he doesn't believe what he's saying. He knows I'm a killer. He will always know. But I wouldn't hurt a child. I wouldn't.

Baldy growls deep in his chest.

Is that a threat?

A warning?

I can see the larger picture now, though. If I want to keep him, I have to take all of Harvey's history as my own. I have to become his story. I have to take on that burden and understand that beating. I'm the pot, the motherfucking cauldron, that has to take on all of him.

Fuck.

I'm not sure I can do that.

"Harvey, come here." My voice sounds shrill and panicky. I try to breathe. "Harvey." My voice is sharp and blunt. *Sharp* and *blunt*, two words when used together that can only describe a paradox—or a weapon—some prehistoric tool sharpened on one edge.

I need one of those.

I look at Rex. I'm going to run. I'm going to grab Harvey and run. I hope Rex knows that. I hope he's on my side in this but I can't tell from his face. I wish he would say something.

"Everyone should get some rest," Sister Azzie says in her sweet, perky little voice. "The path we seek will be more easily revealed in the morning light."

I am not staying here. No fucking way. Not with these people.

"Tomorrow we'll have a look at that car of yours and see what we can do."

Rex puts his hand on my shoulder. "It'll be all right, Kitty. We can't go nowhere without getting Linda fixed up."

Fuck, I forgot all about that. We're trapped here. "Harvey." This time I say his name like a normal person rather than some raving madwoman.

The priest lets go of him and he runs to my side. I scoop him up and hold on to him. He feels plumper, more like a kid should. Maybe I'm squeezing too tight.

"That's an excellent idea, Sister." The priest comes at me and pats Harvey's shoulder.

Harvey wails like the father's touch burns.

Rex flinches. Would he punch a priest for me?

I clutch Harvey tighter. He is not taking this kid from me.

"We'll talk more in the morning."

We'll get the fuck out of here in the morning, you mean. I walk with Harvey to our room. It's only a few steps. I run my hand along the wall to feel for the light switch. I can't find it. I put Harvey down. "Stay right here. Close to me." I can't see anything in the room and I can't find the damned light switch. It occurs to me that they don't have electricity. I open the curtain. In the light from the fire, I see Rex and the father with their heads tilted together. Rex better not be telling him anything. He better fucking not.

He would never do that, but how would I know? They are probably just talking about the car. Guys talk about cars a lot.

I put Harvey on his little cot. Baldy hops up next to him and curls up. "Who hit you?" I ask the kid. "Did your father do that?" He tilts his head downward. He's assented. I'm sure of it.

My mind winds up tighter and tighter like an old-fashioned watch. I hesitate for a second. Should I kiss the kid? Hug him? I lie down on the bed without doing either. If that priest causes trouble, I'll get Harvey to say the father hit him. *His* father, *the* father, the difference is miniscule. I'm sure I can get Harvey to say it. That'll show that son of a bitch for trying to take Harvey.

I watch the light from the fire flicker on the walls. What the hell is Rex talking to that priest about?

The minute I think it, Rex walks through the door. He closes it and half the light disappears.

"Lock it," I say.

Rex looks around for a minute. "Got no lock."

"Figures."

Rex sits on the edge of the bed and takes off first one boot then the other.

"Hey, Rex."

"Yeah?"

Rex lies down beside me on the bed. He is as rigid as a pool cue. He doesn't kiss me or hug me or anything at all. I wouldn't have minded. What could that priest have possibly said to him? I wanted to know but I was afraid to ask.

"Why do you think they'd build a big fire like that?"

"Probably it keeps the wolves away."

TEN

Light blazes in through the window, as hot and corporeal as boiling oil. I don't know how long I've been lying in this old-fashioned bed with the sun on my face. I am blinded by the black afterimage of its radiance. How did that happen through my closed eyelids? I throw out my arm. I'm alone in the bed. Last thing I remember, I'd been listening to Rex's snoring. I jump up. I've been sleeping!

"Harvey!" I can't see him. Can't see through the black hole in my vision. My voice is a croak. My throat feels like sandpaper. "Harvey."

I stumble through the open door out into the courtyard. The air, thick with the smell of charred wood, burns my nostrils and throat. I need water. I need Harvey and Rex and I need to get the fuck out of here.

I blink and blink until my vision clears. Harvey and Baldy are across the courtyard. They are misshapen silhouettes, like a boy and his dog lawn ornaments made without a pattern, against the washed-out white of the sky.

I run to them. The charred air is heavy in my chest. "What the hell are you doing?" I yell as I run. It comes out sounding like some raspy old train station bitch yelling about the end of the world to passersby. "You scared the crap out of me," I gasp as I grab Harvey and pull him to me.

He squirms to get free.

I let him go. Maybe I overreacted a little. My mom was always doing that. If I was ten minutes late getting home from school, she acted like I'd been taken hostage by a pedophile. I always hated that crap when I was a kid. I guess I got it from her.

Fuck.

I always said I was never going to do that if I ever had a kid.

I completely get it, though. This was how my mom felt, every time.

"Where'd you get water?" I ask Harvey, who's floating an origami boat in a basin of grimy water.

"From the well." He waves his arm. He laughs and the sound of it echoes in a hollow, creepy way.

Why is that funny?

Beyond the sheds that look like they might have held garden tools or bicycles or something, all I see is the irregular checkerboard of Joshua trees and tufts of desert grass spreading out to infinity. No well. I want, I *need*, water.

"Show me." I take Harvey's hand and pull him to his feet, not giving him time to protest.

Baldy growls and I could swear his eyes flash red. Must be the light hitting the inside of his eyes just right.

Don't dog eyes glow green? Or maybe it's red.

Harvey runs through the gap between a shed and one of the larger buildings, dragging me with him.

He drops my hand and rushes up to a little brick well that looks just like an illustration from a book of nursery rhymes. He jumps up on the edge and throws his leg over.

"No!"

I lunge for him and pull him off the ledge. I know I said I wouldn't act like that anymore, but I can't stop myself.

Do all kids jump like that? He seemed to bounce once and fly. It wasn't so long ago that I was a kid. I could never do that, I don't think.

Once he is safely on the ground, I notice the scales under my feet. They cover the ground like cherry blossom petals. Weird place for fish scales to be. A pail dangles at the end of a rope with a ladle hanging from it. Is that sanitary? My throat is so dry, I don't care.

As I am drinking, Harvey takes off running.

Fuck.

Kids are kind of a pain in the ass.

Out in front of the semicircle of mission buildings, the priest leans under the hood of Rex's car.

Bastard.

I hate that guy. He thinks he can just tell me what to do. Fucking priest thinks he's going to be *my* moral compass, he's got another thing coming. His neck looks too long as he's leaning over the engine, like a lizard or something. I think about the logistics of slamming the hood on his head. Would that even kill a guy? Or would he just push it up and be seriously pissed about it. You never can tell about things like that. TV makes it look like one little bonk on the head and down they go. I've got the scar from where my broken rib poked through my skin to prove that's not the case.

Harvey runs right up to Rex, which means he also runs right up to the priest.

Fucking kid.

Doesn't he know that priest is the enemy? The priest is trying to take Harvey away. Harvey acts like he isn't even scared. Maybe he's got faith that I will protect him. I wish I had that kind of faith.

I hurry over to where they're working. Not too fast though. I'm not going to let that son of a bitch know I'm worried.

"Hey," I say.

"Hey, Kitty. Listen to this." Rex grins real big and cranks the engine. It roars and then settles down to a hum like the purr of a happy cat.

Rex jumps out of the driver's seat. "Whoo! Whoo! On the road again. Mexico, here we come."

"Yay!" I say without any sarcasm for the first time ever in my life.

I mean it.

Fucking yay!

I can't wait to get out of this place.

The priest wipes his hands on a rag. He shakes his head like he's especially sad as he grabs his cane. Where the hell did that come from? Damn priests and their conjuring abilities. His eyes settle on Harvey and stay there.

"The boy will be staying here with us, like we agreed."

"No, no, we did not agree." My voice warbles and sounds like I'm unsure of myself.

I'm not.

The father puts his hands on Harvey.

I spring. I clutch Harvey and pull him away.

The priest swings his cane. It connects with the bridge of my nose. A sharp white pain shoots through my skull. I can't see through the milky-white opacity of agony.

I can hear though.

POP! POP! The sound expands like an earache. It's followed by an ominous thud of a body hitting the ground.

An acrid, sulfurous smell envelopes me as my vision clears.

The father lies in the sand. There's a gaping hole where his forehead should be.

Rex doesn't look right. Sweat drips from his face. He's holding the gun. His hand is shaking.

Even Baldy the dog looks shocked by Rex's behavior.

I snatch Harvey up and cover his eyes. I run with him to the car.

"Go!"

Rex takes too long to react. He stares at the fallen priest. All of him is shaking like he's having a seizure. Now is not the time for that.

A dark shadow crosses in front of the sun. Blocks the

light like an eclipse. A *thwap, thwap, thwap* sound fills the air. Giant beating wings.

Harvey knocks my hand away from his eyes.

"Azrael flies," he says in that deep too-old voice.

"Let's go!" I shriek.

ELEVEN

One August when I was a kid, our central air broke down. It was hot like I'd never experienced before. Me and my mom lay on the tile floor in the kitchen and stayed perfectly still. It didn't help much. The window was open and I could hear the neighbor's dog yapping and the zoom of cars passing by. The yellow gingham curtain didn't move a bit. The wind chimes with the silver bird heads on tubes like whistles didn't stir. It was take-your-breath-away hot.

My mom told me a story about a dog that was stolen from his home and sent in a crate to the Yukon to be a sled dog. She told me that story because it had a lot of snow in it and I guess she thought that would make the heat easier to bear. It was cool that she tried something creative like that.

That night my dad came home with a new air conditioner. All the stores around our house had sold out of air conditioners because of the heat wave and he was late because he went all over the place looking for one. That was a nice sentiment and all, but it didn't matter. We'd already done the suffering, his good intentions didn't take any of that away. I remember wanting to bite and scratch and kick him. My mom had to hold me back. I was a kid but I was pretty sure I could have done some damage if she'd let go of me.

I was overreacting back then. It wasn't like the heat was life-threatening.

The heat is life-threatening now. Baldy the dog is panting harder than I've ever seen a dog pant. He keeps saying, *water*, over and over. It's seriously creeping me out. I know dogs can't talk. I know it. But I completely understand this one.

Harvey was crying earlier. He stopped when I yelled at him. I probably shouldn't have done that, but fuck, I know it's hot, you don't have to keep saying it. He didn't exactly stop the second I yelled. He, in fact, cried even harder, then climbed down on the floor where I can't see him. He sobbed and heaved and probably lost tons of water from his body. Add that to the list of shit not to do to a kid. Seriously, how is it possible to fuck up so much in just one day? I'm feeling kind of like I might want to forgive my parents for some of the things they did because, damn. Kids seem like an unwinnable game. How are there even still people on earth? I wish Harvey was crying now because then I'd at least know...

Fuck.

I think we're going to die. I can't see an alternative.

Linda is barely moving. Whatever Rex and the priest fixed didn't stay fixed for long. The hot tar, burning-plastic smell gags me. Linda is probably going to be the first of us to go.

I'm going to miss her. She feels like a friend.

The lump from the fly bite on Rex's neck looks really bad. It's swollen to the size of a slider from White Castle. The part where he was bitten is oozing and turning purple. The edges of the wound look like liver. There's another bite on his cheek that's starting to puff up too. The veins in his neck stand out too much from the skin. He's not the right color. His face is a bluish shade of gray I've only seen on really old homeless guys on the coldest days of winter.

I'm driving because Rex needs to sleep. *Needs to sleep* might not be exactly the right way to say it. Sleeping isn't really optional with Rex. I think he might be unconscious, but I don't know how to tell for sure. His chest is rising and falling, so there's that at least. He needs water, food, a doctor.

I'm thirstier than I can ever remember. And I don't want to look, but I know my face is burned. It's going to take a whole lot of lotion to cure sunburn that hurts as much as this one. Sunburn seems almost stupid to think about. But I do, but only a little.

The hum of flies is not quite as loud as the grind and ping of Linda's engine. I swat them away but they crawl over Rex like he's already dead. That's the most horrible sight I've ever seen. And I've seen some horrible shit. All I have to do is swat them away. The flies aren't attached to him. They aren't part of him. But it seems like they are. It seems like they're rising by spontaneous generation from his body. But that's crazy. No one has believed in spontaneous generation since the seventeenth century when Louis Pasteur proved that tapeworms didn't come from rotten meat. I can see why people believed that theory for so long though. If people look at rotten meat long enough, they're bound to see something move.

"Harvey," I call out as I twist my head around and look where he's huddled on the floor behind Rex's seat.

"It's too hot, Kitty. This body must have water."

Why this kid couldn't say *I'm thirsty* like an ordinary kid is a mystery to me.

"I know, honey," I say real sweet and patient because it wouldn't kill me for once in my fucking life to be kind. I'm not the monster I thought I was, I guess. Monsters don't feel this bad about other people. Fine fucking time to learn this little fact about myself. "I'm going to figure something out real soon."

That's a lie even though I said I'd never lie to my kid like my parents did. I get why they did it now. If the truth is horrible, telling it is the same as hitting the kid. It's so very clear to me that I can't imagine why I was so angry about my parents' lies. They were shielding me from the blows.

I can't decide if I should tell Harvey the story about the

dog that gets captured and taken to the Yukon to become a sled dog. I try to remember if hearing a story about snow makes it feel cooler. I can almost feel the tile floor of my old kitchen on my cheek.

That story stuck with me long after my mother told it to me. The thing I remember most about that story was how mean the people were to the dog. How no matter where he went, the people were fucking horrible. The man with the red sweater beat him and another man who was trying to be good ended up starving the dog because he was stupid. The dog went wild. That was even the name of the book.

My mother was just trying to help me get through a heat wave. There was no way she could know how a story about a dog in the snow would get into my head. There was no way she could have known that I'd follow the wolf into the woods. I decided not to tell Harvey the story of *The Call of the Wild*. That's not a fucking story for kids.

I hear a droning sound. It's not the flies and it's not Linda. It comes from behind a rise in the desert floor. Not even on a road, just coming out of the desert like they're part of it, are four riders on motorcycles.

A girl who hadn't followed the wolf into the wild might have been relieved to see them.

I wasn't that girl. This couldn't be good.

The panic wave laps at me.

Washes over me.

Crests.

Whatever is going to happen is going to happen.

It'll be over soon.

TWELVE

They are friendly—friends.

The four.

I truly did not expect this.

Truly.

I have to rethink my expectations of people. I thought I was a good judge. Maybe I'm not.

They are costumed superheroes without capes; they each have their color. The red rider is fierce, fierce the way dogs in a dogfight are. Her face is hard and sharp with a scar from chin to cheek. She expels words like they're bullets while she heaves Rex onto her bike. The black rider is as thin as any holocaust survivor. His ragged pants remind me of a cartoon I liked as a kid, *The Christmas Carole*. The black rider looks like the children *Want* or *Woe* that hide in the cloak of Christmas Future. He lifts Baldy the dog onto his bike. The dog is as thin as the black rider. He looks starved to the point that he resembles a purse with bones. He doesn't look like a living thing. Now that I think about it, I don't think I fed him even once...except the ice cream. I am going to cry. I am crying. It doesn't matter now. The white rider wears a vest with a blood red X painted or stitched on his chest. His arms, pocked and mangled by scars, carry Harvey gently like he's broken, like I broke him. Flies swarm around them. Around us all. I can't describe the color of the rider who hoists me onto his bike. I can't pin down the name of it. It's watery like champagne, not green, not gray. It's pale. That's not a color.

I ride on the bike of an indescribable color. It feels like

riding a horse. I know it isn't, but the bumps feel like gal-
lops. I think I may have faded in and out for a while as I
cling to the rider. Time moves fast, slow, fast again.

They saved us—are saving us—as much as that's still
possible. I trust them. I have no other choice. I can see the
limp bodies of Baldy and Harvey and Rex draped over the
other riders. I wonder where they are taking us. I wonder
about this for as long as I can.

THE SALTON SEA

Located directly on the San Andreas Fault in California's Coachella Valley, the Salton Sea is a shallow, saline, endorheicEndorheic basin. Created in 1905 when a flood overwhelmed the California Development Company's efforts to divert the Colorado River, the Salton Sea is the largest lake in California. Although it varies depending on rainfall and runoff, the sea is approximately 525 square miles. The salinity of the lake, at 44 grams per liter, is greater than the Pacific Ocean. Because it has no outlet, salinity increases 1 percent per year.

In the 1950s, the resort towns of Salton City, Desert Shores and Bombay Beach enjoyed an influx of visitors. In less than a decade, fertilizer runoff and increasing salinity produced ideal conditions for algae bloom. The elevated bacterial levels caused by the bloom resulted in perennial fish and wildlife die-off. The combination of summer temperatures that often reach 120 degrees, foul smells of algae die-off detectable for hundreds of miles, and a series of floods that destroyed most of the tourist attractions encouraged people to find other recreational waters. The towns on the shore of the Salton Sea became and remain ghost towns.

THIRTEEN

Once I tried to cook a whole fish in foil on the grill. The fish was expensive. I went to a fish market to buy it. The guy behind the counter wrapped it in white waxy paper. I bought all sorts of special herbs and a whole case of champagne. I stole a credit card. It was the first time I ever did. I wanted to make a special celebration dinner for Joey's birthday because he was having a really bad go of things. At the time, I'm pretty sure I convinced myself I was planning a party. I was going to call up everyone we went to school with and invite them over. But honestly I think I knew all along it was only ever going to be just us two. There was no way we could ever go back there. Not after what Joey did. Our friends were dead to us. That old life was gone for good. In retrospect, buying the case of champagne was probably where I made my first mistake. The second was drinking it with an Oxy chaser. I can't reliably recount what happened that weekend. But the next day that I can remember was after Joey was gone. That day I lifted the cover on the grill. The fish I bought for us looked up at me with milky maggot-filled eyes.

I smell that very same smell now. I'm afraid to open my eyes because I have no idea where I could possibly be and the smell is not a good sign. My head is resting on someone's chest. If I had to guess, I would say I'm lying on Rex's chest. I want to hold on as tight as I can because I know him. If I think too much about it, I'm going to come to the conclusion that I don't know Rex, not really. I hold on tight and try my best not to think. That never does work. But I try. I concentrate on the buzz around my head.

I wish Joey hadn't cut himself that one last time while I was passed out. If I'd been a better friend, a better person, I'd have been there for him.

I miss him.

Maybe Joey did the right thing. He was going to go to jail. He killed that son-of-a bitch and it was just a matter of time before he got caught. Jail would have most certainly killed him. He was small, fragile. There was no other way to escape.

Flies.

The tickle of tiny legs on me make me want to thrash and flail.

But I don't.

Outside I hear a voice. Not a conversation, just a single voice. I must be inside because the voice sounds like it's on the other side of a window. But inside where? I still don't want to look.

The voice belongs to the red rider. The woman. She sounds like she's giving a speech. It's familiar, like something I should have learned in school. Joan of Arc, maybe? Shakespeare?

She says something about unjust wars and mutual destruction. Her words sound ominous. Even if she's only screwing around, it does not sound good.

"Rex, are you awake?"

"That I am, Kitty."

The knot inside me loosens up a little. I love Rex. And maybe that's just the desperation stirring my emotions like a blender on high, but I do. I love him like he's the last man on earth.

Fuck. I hope that's not the case.

"Where are we, Rex?"

"Sounds like we're in church. That wouldn't be the worst thing." Rex's voice is croaky and muffled. "I could use a prayer."

Rex sounds like he's talking with a sock in his mouth. I don't want to look, but I can't just lie here like some kind of girly bitch cringing in fear.

I open my eyes. I purposely don't look at Rex's face. This is not a church. It could be the belly of a whale though. We're lying on some rotted old mattress. It's mostly made up of brown coils of wire with tufts of cotton that look like it needs to be ginned clinging to the wires. It's covered here and there by scraps of stiff, piss-yellow fabric. It's on the floor of the rusted and shattered remains of one of those '50s-style campers that always appear on postcards for sale along Route 66. What the fuck happened to this thing? It's not burned, but it's decimated. Its crippled rib spines are covered with a tarp. The sun shining through the gaps in the tarp falls on some sparkling, ganglious growths. Salt. Salt is encrusted on everything.

"You okay?" Rex asks me. He does not sound good.

"Yeah, I think so," I say. I turn my head so I can see him. It takes everything I've got. His face is swollen twice as big as it should be. His eyes are hidden behind mounds of purplish swollen flesh. His lips are cracked and caked with rust-brown blood. The boils on his neck and chest and cheek have burst. White snakes of pus ooze from him.

I scream just a little and pull away. I'm proud of myself for not screaming more. Not pus, maggots. The tiny white worms curl and uncurl into themselves. It is seriously the most disgusting thing I've ever seen, but for some reason it doesn't seem like it's part of Rex. *He* doesn't disgust me. It's not his fault.

It's mine.

Fuck.

This is seriously bad. Is it even possible to get better once you've got maggots?

"I'm going to help you, Rex. I am, somehow."

"Thanks, Kitty. I appreciate that."

"Can you get up?" I ask as I push myself to my knees. I feel shaky. Maybe I'm going to pass out. But I don't. I grab Rex's arm and lift him. His flesh feels spongy and damp. But he's getting up. He's getting up on unsteady legs. The wound on his face weeps down his cheek. He can stand, though, as long as he leans on me.

"Hey, Kitty."

"Yeah?"

"You know that voice inside that tells you what's right and what's wrong?"

We shuffle across the uneven floor to the metal door. A scrap of red and white gingham is taped over the window with a strip of salty duct tape. Even in its better days this camper probably wasn't all that great.

"No, Rex. No, I do not." The door screeches like a raccoon when I kick it open. Somehow we make it down the metal steps without falling.

Rex doesn't look any better in direct light. He looks worse in fact. Much, much worse.

Salt-covered weeds crunch under my feet. Rex leans against me, heavy as a wet sandbag. All around us there are weird lumps of campers and building and piles of wood. They're spaced out like this place used to be a neighborhood.

It's not a neighborhood now.

"Everyone hears the voice," Rex says. He's not breathing right. It's shallow and coming in little gasps. "That's what makes you human."

We're at the beach. But it's like no beach I've ever seen. The water spreads as far as I can see. Water, that's what we need. That's what Rex needs. But this water looks thick, jellylike. It has a reddish tinge that reminds me of blood. The waves, what passes for waves, wiggle like Jell-O shooters. Along the shore, from the last crumbled building to the edge of the water, lies a blanket of decay. Fish, birds, creatures that climbed out of the ooze and never fully formed lay in a thick decaying blanket. Is it the ocean? Did we ride that far? Has something unimaginably horrible happened in the world while I slept?

The riders sit around a fire in the skeleton of a boat that looks like it may never have been seaworthy.

"We now hold out to you wars which contain the glorious reward of martyrdom, which will retain that title of praise now and forever." The red rider stands on the ledge of the crumbling boat. She looks like a warrior. She is war.

Fuck.

I get it now.

"You got to listen to that voice now, Kitty. You've got to do what it says. That's God telling you what to do."

I stumble toward the riders. Curls of black smoke rise from their fire like phantoms. Which culture told fortunes with smoke? It makes sense that they'd do that. There seems to be meaning in the shapes and billows of black as it moves through the gray air.

"I don't have that voice, Rex. I just don't have it."

His body sags. Grows heavier.

"I'm really sorry."

Rex stumbles. I grab his arm and hold it tight.

"Kitty, you remember how I told you I got a second chance?"

"Yeah."

"I don't think I did."

"You're going to be fine, Rex. We're going to get you some help."

"I want to tell you something before the next part starts."

Rex clutches me and makes me stop.

"What is it, Rex?"

The air is as hot as the inside of an oven. It's too hot for a fire but still the riders lounge around theirs inside the broken-down boat.

"I shot that old woman when I stole her boy's car. Left her on the floor of her house."

My mouth falls open. Of all the things I've seen and done, why would this be shocking?

"I stepped over her for two weeks until I couldn't stand to look at her no more. I'm sorry for that."

"The picture in your suitcase?"

"That's her."

The nasty water laps at the shore—and everything is encrusted and sparkling with salt. I liked the Rex I used to know better. But I *love* this Rex. The real one. He gave me his truth.

I look down at the shirt that I'm wearing, Rex's shirt. It's tattered and not as white as it was. I lock onto the monogramed *B*. "What's your real name?"

He can't be a Bill or a Bob. Maybe Bronson, Broderick, Bruce?

"That's not my shirt," he says.

Baldy, the world's ugliest dog, crouches on the rocky beach. He's opening his mouth like he would if he were yapping, but only a croak comes out. He's wiggling and squirming to get to the water—going crazy.

Harvey, a tiny silhouette of Harvey, is served up on the white-hot plate of the setting sun. He's in the water. He's on the water. He's walking on water!

My insides seize up. A voice in my head shrieks, *Save the boy*!

FOURTEEN

Harvey! I rush through the dead, decayed things and plunge into the salty muck of the sea. As the shriek leaves my throat, he sinks as though my lack of faith deflated him. I've never had faith in anything.

I dive in, swim. The salt and the putrid rot in the air burns my lungs. I can't see him. I see only the spot where he used to be.

I force my arms and legs to move the way I learned in summer camp all those years ago. Back when swimming wasn't a life-or-death thing.

Where is he! Where is he! I thrash in the water. This is where he should be. The water buoys me and makes me unnaturally light. This is not the way the world works. Where is he? I can't make myself sink. But Rex was right about one thing: there is a voice in my head. It screams: *Save the boy!*

That is my mission. My only task. The one thing I must accomplish.

Bobbing on the surface, out of my reach, I see a mass of brown seaweed. His hair!

Save the boy! Save him! Save him. The voice swells. A hymn all-encompassing. I concentrate my thrashing, corral it into forward motion with the force of my will.

Finally, I reach him. Plunge my fingers into the mass of his hair and pull his head up. His eyes are staring, not blinking. What is he looking at! What does he see?

I throw my arm around his chest and under his arm. Save him!

The words chorus in my head.

"Help!" I scream, but I can't see the riders, or Rex or—the shore! It's all become a blur of gray-white beach, sky and water. It's all of a thing.

Harvey isn't warm—or cool. He's exactly the same temperature as the water. He's heavy like a sponge. Like he's joined the sea in trying to thwart me in my impossible task. I must capture and carry this one amorphous shifting bundle of water drops to safety.

I must save him!

I kick as hard as I've ever kicked and pull with my free arm. No matter what I do, it's not fast enough. Harvey isn't breathing. I push the thought away. I am breathing—breathing enough for us both. And swimming and pulling him closer toward what must be land. It must be.

The skeletal shape of the boat, the husk of the rusted camper, the neighborhood of collapsed houses wavers into view.

Land.

I thrust a leg down. My foot hits rock and sand.

I heave Harvey up on my shoulder. And run. As much as running is possible through the gelatinous spume and chum. A sharp stone or maybe a broken bottle slices my foot. I'm aware of the pain. Of the salt in the wound, but still I push on.

I am breathing.

"Rex!"

I see him slumped against the shell of the boat. He doesn't move. He can't help me. I don't think I can help him.

Not anymore.

Save the boy! The words ring in my ears. Something strange happens to the way I see. I'm above it all looking down. I see what I have to do!

Baldy is worked up into a frothing frenzy of disjointed bones and lizard-like skin. His barks hit the air as hard as gunshots.

I drop Harvey onto the beach and fall down beside him. One knee lands in a spot free of rotting fish corpses.

One doesn't.

I pry Harvey's mouth open. Feel for foreign objects. I remember this. I remember. His tongue is too large for a child. Maybe it was always that way. I never checked. I should have checked. I should have known him better.

His mouth is salty. As salty as the last of the popcorn in an extra-large tub. I'm breathing. He's breathing. I think he's breathing. I blow in the air and push it out. That's breathing. It has to be.

"I must save him," I yell between breaths. His, mine. He must breathe.

Baldy's barking ceases.

The hymn floods over me.

Save him. Save him.

The dog looks in my eyes like a human would. He knows I'm the one.

"I'm going to save him."

Baldy turns away. He scrabbles across the debris-strewn beach and falls on his side close but not touching Rex, like he's guarding him. Like he's telling me he's got my back.

"I'm going to save him," I say again to the dog.

The rider tilts his head in the affirmative. He understands. He's the only one left. Where have they gone? The Black, the Red and the White riders. Did they go for help? Even as the idea comes into my head, I know it's wrong.

I can see the whole picture. They've gone to the four corners of the earth to spread their pestilence, plague and discord.

The last rider throws his leg over his bike and revs up the engine. I know what I'm supposed to do.

I am the agent of change.

I must take Harvey where he belongs.

LOS ANGELES

In 1781, a group of eleven families settled along a river in an area the Spanish were attempting to cultivate as a land route to the Port of Monterrey. Felipe de Neve, governor of Spanish California, named the settlement El Pueblo Sobre el Rio de Nuestra Señora la Reina de los Angeles del Río de Porciúncula. Almost immediately, the name was shortened.

For most of its existence, Los Angeles was a sleepy, small town on the Pacific Coast. An opportune conflagration of oil, water, railroads, shipping, immigrants and moving pictures exploded to make Los Angeles the third largest metropolitan economy in the world with a population of 13 million, and a GDP higher than the countries of Belgium, Saudi Arabia, Norway and Taiwan.

Although most famous for movie production, Los Angeles is the largest manufacturing center in the western U.S. The ports of Los Angeles and Long Beach are among the busiest in the world. Forty percent of all goods on the planet pass through Los Angeles. The Centers for Disease Control and U.S. Department of Homeland Security warnings indicate that an airborne pathogen passing through the transportation network of Los Angeles would be difficult if not impossible to contain.

FIFTEEN

The air isn't salty anymore. It's thin and tinged with smoke and exhaust and it's blowing by so fast I'm afraid it will steal my breath. I clutch Harvey to my chest. He's pressed between me and the rider. The bike roars under us. Pistons stroke hard and methodical like industry, progress. The metal is hot on my bare, ravaged feet. The power feels barely contained. We careen from lane to lane as the L.A. skyline twinkles into view. I expect any minute to skid and roll. I brace for the burn of asphalt on my face, the crush and smear of oncoming traffic.

Harvey isn't as heavy as he was. He's light, in fact. It's like the air is sucking away all the moisture he soaked up in the Salton Sea. That's where we'd been. I saw a billboard. We weren't in the postapocalyptic world, just in some weird ghost town alongside some messed-up manmade lake. I don't feel better because of that revelation. I have faith that I was shown a vision of our future. I believe that. I do.

Harvey isn't heavy anymore. I haven't been breathing for him since we've been riding. I'd like to think he's doing it for himself. Or that we're going fast enough...

No.

I know.

I know, but I can't look at him.

I can't.

I've never been a good person. I see that now. I'm a killer, a liar, a cheat. How could I be so stupid to think I could change? That I could be good just this one time.

I found the boy at a crossroads after killing a man, *two*, in cold blood. The signs were there all along. I never believed in all that shit before. Guess that was stupid.

I'm not just bad. I'm not just criminal. I'm evil.

Fuck.

I'm the agent of evil. I don't think I'm going to hell, though. I'm pretty sure I've brought it to earth.

I have to look at the boy. I have to know what I've done.

I feel the panic lapping at me. I let it rush in—wash over me—recede.

Whatever is going to happen is going to happen.

I look.

Harvey isn't a boy anymore. He's still in the shape of a boy, more or less. But he's dry, desiccated. I clutch him to me. I wanted more than anything I've ever wanted to save him.

I didn't.

We, the pale rider and me, slow as we reach the core of the city.

Golden morning light blooms over the spires of office towers and warehouses and shops. Its light flames in their windows. Cars stream above and below us in concrete flues. It's a Disneyland of labor, constructed, perfected. The vehicles move individually but not in their multitude, like water in a river is water but also a river.

White lights approach; red recede into the pink dawn. This is what the word *multitude* means.

We stop as the river snarls. I must put my feet on the ground.

He dissolves in my arms. His little face, arms, tiny child fingers with perfect little nails crumble. The sensation is worse than the worst nightmare of losing teeth or limbs, or killing kittens by forgetting to feed them. My heart is on the outside, exposed. No one told me a child could cause this pain. I can only hold on. Hold on to nothing. I can't stop him from coming apart. Dispersing.

A gray cloud of particulate matter—an immense swarm of flies—assault the vivid morning sky of Los Angeles. It is vast, unbounded, immeasurable. This is the essence of the word *disaster*.

Pestilence, War, Famine—Death.

I am done for.

But worse, somehow, that I never would have understood before today—

WE—

Are done for.

The dark cloud of the boy, *my boy*, descends on L.A.

Whatever is going to happen is going to happen.

ACKNOWLEDGEMENTS

Thank you to Matthew for his help and patience. And to Keri Kelley and Johnny Worthen for their help on early drafts.

About the Author

Kate is a student of all things scary and when she isn't writing she loves to collect objects for her cabinet of curiosities, research obscure and strange historical figures and photograph weirdness in Southern California where she lives with a very nice man and two little dogs who are also very nice but could behave a little bit better.

Links to her novel *Candy House* published by Evil Jester Press and anthologies containing stories of hers can be found on her website: katejonez.com